BOULE DE SUIF

AND OTHER STORIES

Boule de Suif and Other Stories

by

Guy de Maupassant

Translated and Edited
by Ernest Boyd

Short Story Index Reprint Series

BOOKS FOR LIBRARIES PRESS
FREEPORT, NEW YORK

Originally published as Volume 1 of the
Collected Novels and Stories of Guy de Maupassant

Reprinted 1971 by arrangement

INTERNATIONAL STANDARD BOOK NUMBER:
0-8369-3898-4

LIBRARY OF CONGRESS CATALOG CARD NUMBER:
76-157786

PRINTED IN THE UNITED STATES OF AMERICA

CONTENTS

BOULE DE SUIF

FOR several days in succession straggling remnants of the routed army had passed through the town. They were not the regular army, but a disjointed rabble, the men unshaven and dirty, their uniforms in tatters, slouching along without regimental colors, without order — worn out, broken down, incapable of thought or resolution, marching from pure habit and dropping with fatigue the moment they stopped. The majority belonged to the militia, men of peaceful pursuits, retired from business, sinking under the weight of their accoutrements; quick-witted little militiamen as prone to terror as they were to enthusiasm, as ready to attack as they were to fly; and here and there a few red trousers, remnants of a company mowed down in one of the big battles; sombre-coated artillerymen, side by side with these various uniforms of the infantry, and now and then the glittering helmet of a heavily booted dragoon who followed with difficulty the march of the lighter-footed soldiers of the line.

Companies of franc-tireurs, heroically named "Avengers of the Defeat," "Citizens of the Tomb," "Companions in Death," passed in their turn, looking like a horde of bandits.

Their chiefs — formerly drapers or corn-dealers,

retired soap-boilers or suet-refiners, temporary heroes, created officers for their money or the length of their moustaches, heaped with arms, flannels, and gold lace — talked loudly, discussed plans of campaign, and gave you to understand that they were the sole support of France in her death-agony; but they were generally in terror of their own soldiers, gallows birds, most of them brave to fool-hardiness, all of them given to pillage and debauchery.

Report said that the Prussians were about to enter Rouen. The National Guard, which for two months past had made the most careful reconnoitreings in the neighbouring wood, even to the extent of occasionally shooting their own sentries and putting themselves in battle array if a rabbit stirred in the brushwood, had now retired to their domestic hearths; their arms, their uniforms, all the murderous apparatus with which they had been wont to strike terror to the hearts of all beholders for three leagues round, had vanished.

Finally, the last of the French soldiery crossed the Seine on their way to Pont-Audemer by Saint Sever and Bourg-Achard; and then, last of all, came their despairing general tramping on foot between two orderlies, powerless to attempt any action with these disjointed fragments of his forces, himself utterly dazed and bewildered by the downfall of a people accustomed to victory and now so disastrously beaten in spite of its traditional bravery.

After that a profound calm, the silence of terrified suspense, fell over the city. Many a rotund bourgeois, emasculated by a purely commercial life, awaited the arrival of the victors with anxiety, trembling lest their meat-skewers and kitchen carving-knives should come under the category of arms.

Life seemed to have come to a standstill, the shops were closed, the streets silent. From time to time an inhabitant, intimidated by their silence, would flit rapidly along the pavement, keeping close to the walls.

In this anguish of suspense, men longed for the coming of the enemy.

In the latter part of the day following the departure of the French troops, some Uhlans, appearing from goodness knows where, traversed the city hastily. A little later, a black mass descended from the direction of Sainte-Catherine, while two more invading torrents poured in from the roads from Darnetal and Boisguillaume. The advance guards of the three corps converged at the same moment into the square of the Hotel de Ville, while battalion after battalion of the German army wound in through the adjacent streets, making the pavement ring under their heavy rhythmic tramp.

Orders shouted in strange and guttural tones were echoed back by the apparently dead and deserted houses, while from behind the closed shutters eyes peered furtively at the conquerors, masters by right of might, of the city and the lives and fortunes of its inhabitants. The people in their darkened dwellings fell a prey to the helpless bewilderment which comes over men before the floods, the devastating upheavals of the earth, against which all wisdom and all force are unavailing. The same phenomenon occurs each time that the established order of things is overthrown, when public security is at an end, and when all that the laws of man or of nature protect is at the mercy of some blind elemental force. The earthquake burying an entire population under its falling houses; the flood that carries away the drowned body of the peasant with the carcasses of his cattle and the beams torn from his roof-tree; or the victorious army massacring those who defend their lives, and making prisoners of the rest — pillaging in the name of the sword, and thanking God to the roar of cannon — are so many appalling scourges which overthrow all faith in eternal justice, all the confidence we are taught to place in the protection of Providence and the reason of man.

Small detachments now began knocking at the doors and then disappearing into the houses. It was the occupation after the invasion. It now behooved the vanquished to make themselves agreeable to the victors.

After a while, the first alarms having subsided, a new sense of tranquillity began to establish itself. In many families the Prussian officer shared the family meals. Not infrequently he was a gentleman, and out of politeness expressed his commiseration with France and his repugnance at having to take part in such a war. They were grateful enough to him for this sentiment — besides, who knew when they might not be glad of his protection? By gaining his good offices one might have fewer men to feed. And why offend a person on whom one was utterly dependent? That would not be bravery but temerity, a quality of which the citizens of Rouen could no longer be accused as in the days of those heroic defences by which the city had made itself famous. Above all, they said, with the unassailable urbanity of the Frenchman, it was surely permissible to be on politely familiar terms in private, provided one held aloof from the foreign soldier in public. In the street, therefore, they ignored one another's existence, but once indoors they were perfectly ready to be friendly, and each evening found the German staying longer at the family fireside.

The town itself gradually regained its wonted aspect. The French inhabitants did not come out much, but the Prussian soldiers swarmed in the streets. For the rest, the blue hussar officers who trailed their mighty implements of death so arrogantly over the pavement did not appear to entertain a vastly deeper grade of contempt for the simple townsfolk than did the officers of the Chasseurs who had drunk in the same cafés the year before. Nevertheless there was a something in the air; something subtle and indefinable, an intolerably unfamiliar atmosphere like a widely diffused odour — the odour of invasion. It filled the private dwellings and the public places, it affected the taste of food, and gave one the impression of being on a journey, far away from home, among barbarous and dangerous tribes.

The conquerors demanded money — a great deal of money. The inhabitants paid and went on paying; for the matter of that, they were rich. But the wealthier a Normandy tradesman becomes, the more keenly he suffers at each sacrifice each time he sees the smallest particle of his fortune pass into the hands of another.

Two or three leagues beyond the town, however, following the course of the river about Croisset, Dieppedalle or Biessard, the sailors and the fishermen would often drag up the swollen corpse of some uniformed German, killed by a knife-thrust or a kick, his head smashed in by a stone, or thrown into the water from some bridge. The slime of the river bed swallowed up many a deed of vengeance, obscure, savage, and legitimate; unknown acts of heroism, silent onslaughts more perilous to the doer than battles in the light of day and without the trumpet blasts of glory.

For hatred of the Alien is always strong enough to arm some intrepid beings who are ready to die for an Idea.

At last, seeing that though the invaders had subjected the city to their inflexible discipline they had not committed any of the horrors with which rumour had accredited them throughout the length of their triumphal progress, the public took courage and the commercial spirit began once more to stir in the hearts of the local tradespeople. Some of them who had grave interests at stake at Havre, then occupied by the French army, purposed trying to reach that port by going overland to Dieppe and there taking ship.

They took advantage of the influence of German officers whose acquaintance they had made, and a passport was obtained from the general in command.

Having therefore engaged a large diligence with four horses for the journey, and ten persons having entered their names at the livery stable office, they resolved to start on the Tuesday morning before daybreak, to avoid all public remark.

For some days already the ground had been hard with frost, and on the Monday, about three o'clock in the afternoon, thick dark clouds coming up from the north brought the snow, which fell without intermission all the evening and during the whole night.

At half past four the travellers were assembled in the courtyard of the Hotel de Normandie, from whence they were to start.

They were all still half asleep, their teeth chattering with cold in spite of their thick wraps. It was difficult to distinguish one from another in the darkness, their heaped-up winter clothing making them look like fat priests in long cassocks. Two of the men, however, recognized each other; they were joined by a third, and they began to talk. "I am taking my wife with me," said one. "So am I." "And I too." The first one added: "We shall not return to Rouen, and if the Prussians come to Havre we shall slip over to England."

They were all like-minded and all had the same project.

Meanwhile there was no sign of the horses being put in. A small lantern carried by a hostler appeared from time to time out of one dark doorway only to vanish instantly into another. There was a stamping of horses' hoofs deadened by the straw of the litter, and the voice of a man speaking to the animal and cursing sounded from the depths of the stables. A faint sound of bells gave evidence of harnessing, and became presently a clear and continuous jingle timed by the movement of the beast, now stopping, now going on again with a brisk shake, and accompanied by the dull tramp of hob-nailed sabots.

A door closed sharply. All sound ceased. The frozen travellers were silent, standing stiff and motionless. A continuous curtain of white snowflakes glistened as it fell to the ground, blotting out the shape of things, powdering everything with an icy froth; and in the utter stillness of the town, quiet and buried under its winter pall, nothing was audible but this faint, fluttering, and indefinable rustle of falling snow — more a sensation than a sound — the intermingling of ethereal atoms seeming to fill space, to cover the world.

The man reappeared with his lantern, dragging after him by a rope a dejected and unwilling horse. He pushed it against the pole, fixed the traces, and was occupied for a long time in buckling the harness, having only the use of one hand as he carried the lantern in the other. As he turned away to fetch the other horse he caught sight of the motionless group of travellers, by this time white with snow. "Why don't you get inside the carriage?" he said, "you would at least be under cover."

It had never occurred to them, and they made a rush for it. The three men packed their wives into the upper end and then got in themselves, after which other distinct and veiled forms took the remaining seats without exchanging a word.

The floor of the vehicle was covered with straw into which the feet sank. The ladies at the end, who had brought little copper charcoal foot-warmers, proceeded to light them, and for some time discussed their merits in subdued tones, repeating to one another things which they had known all their lives.

At last, the diligence having been furnished with six horses instead of four on account of the difficulties of the road, a voice outside asked, "Is everybody here?" A voice from within answered "Yes," and they started.

The conveyance advanced slowly — slowly — the wheels sinking in the snow; the whole vehicle groaned and creaked, the horses slipped, wheezed, and smoked, and the driver's gigantic whip cracked incessantly, flying from side to side, twining and untwining like a slender snake, and cutting sharply across one or other of the six humping backs, which would thereupon straighten up with a more violent effort.

Imperceptibly the day grew. The airy flakes which a traveller — a true-born Rouennais — likened to a shower of cotton, had ceased to fall; a dirty grey light filtered through the heavy thick clouds which served to heighten the dazzling whiteness of the landscape, where now a long line of trees crusted with icicles would appear, now a cottage with a hood of snow.

In the light of this melancholy dawn the occupants of the diligence began to examine one another curiously.

Right at the end, in the best seats, opposite to one another, dozed Madame and Monsieur Loiseau, wholesale wine merchant of the Rue Grand Pont.

The former salesman of a master who had become bankrupt, Loiseau had bought up the stock and made his fortune. He sold very bad wine at very low prices to the small country retail dealers, and enjoyed the reputation among his friends and acquaintances of being an unmitigated rogue, a thorough Norman full of trickery and jovial humour.

His character for knavery was so well established that one evening at the Prefecture, Monsieur Tournel, a man of keen and trenchant wit, author of certain fables and songs — a local celebrity — seeing the ladies growing drowsy, proposed a game of "L'oiseau vole."[1] The pun itself flew through the prefect's reception rooms and afterwards through the town, and for a whole month called up a grin on every face in the province.

Loiseau was himself a noted wag and famous for his jokes both good and bad, and nobody ever mentioned him without adding immediately, "That man, Loiseau, is simply priceless!"

He was of medium height with a balloon-like stomach and a rubicund face framed in grizzled whiskers. His wife — tall, strong, resolute, loud in voice and rapid of decision — represented order and arithmetic in the business, which he enlivened by his jollity and bustling activity.

Beside them, in a more dignified attitude as befitted his superior station, sat Monsieur Carré-Lamadon, a man of weight; an authority on cotton, proprietor of three spinning factories, officer of the Legion of Honour and member of the General Council. All the time of the Empire he had remained leader of a friendly opposition, for the sole pur-

[1] Literally, "The bird flies" — a pun on the verb *voler*, which means both "to fly" and "to steal."

pose of making a better thing out of it when he came round to the cause which he had fought with polite weapons, to use his own expression. Madame Carré-Lamadon, who was much younger than her husband, was the consolation of all officers of good family who might be quartered at the Rouen garrison. She sat there opposite to her husband, very small, very dainty, very pretty, wrapped in her furs, and regarding the lamentable interior of the vehicle with despairing eyes.

Their neighbours, the Count and Countess Hubert de Bréville, bore one of the most ancient and noble names in Normandy. The Count, an elderly gentleman of dignified appearance, did all in his power to accentuate by every artifice of the toilet his natural resemblance to Henri Quatre, who, according to a legend of the utmost glory to the family, had honoured with his royal embraces a Dame de Bréville, whose husband, in consequence, had been made Count and Governor of the province.

A colleague of Monsieur Carré-Lamadon in the General Council, Count Hubert represented the Orleanist faction in the department. The history of his marriage with the daughter of a small tradesman of Nantes had always remained a mystery. But as the Countess had an air of grandeur, understood better than any one else the art of receiving, passed even for having been beloved by one of the sons of Louis Philippe, the neighbouring nobility bowed down to her, and her salon held the first place in the county, the only one which preserved the traditions of old-fashioned gallantry and to which the entrée was difficult.

The fortune of the Brévilles — all in Government Funds — was reported to yield them an income of five hundred thousand francs.

The six passengers occupied the upper end of the conveyance, the representatives of revenued society, serene in the consciousness of its strength — honest well-to-do people possessed of Religion and Principles.

By some strange chance all the women were seated on the same side, the Countess having two Sisters of Mercy for neighbours, wholly occupied in fingering their long rosaries and mumbling Paters and Aves. One of them was old and so deeply pitted with the smallpox that she looked as if she had received a charge of grape-shot full in the face; the other was very shadowy and frail, with a pretty unhealthy little face, a narrow phthisical chest, consumed by that devouring faith which creates martyrs and ecstatics.

Seated opposite to the two nuns were a man and woman who excited a good deal of attention.

The man, who was well known, was Cornudet, "the Democrat," the terror of all respectable, law-abiding people. For twenty years he had dipped his great red beard into the beer mugs of all the democratic cafés. In the company of kindred spirits he had managed to run through a comfortable little fortune inherited from his father, a confectioner, and he looked forward with impatience to the Republic, when he should obtain the well-merited reward for so many revolutionary draughts. On the Fourth of September — probably through some practical joke — he understood that he had been appointed prefect, but on attempting to enter upon his duties the clerks, who had remained sole masters of the offices, refused to recognize him, and he was constrained to retire. For the rest, he was a good fellow, inoffensive and serviceable, and had busied himself with incomparable industry in organizing the defence of the town; had had holes dug all over the plain, cut down all the young trees in the neighbouring woods, scattered pitfalls up and down all the high roads, and at the threatened approach of the enemy — satisfied with his preparations — had fallen back with all haste on the town. He now considered that he would be more useful in Havre, where fresh entrenchments would soon become necessary.

The woman, one of the so-called "gay" sisterhood, was noted for her precocious stoutness, which had gained her the nickname of "Boule de Suif" — "ball of fat." She was a little roly-poly creature, cushioned with fat, with podgy fingers squeezed in at the joints like rows of thick, short sausages; her skin tightly stretched and shiny, her bust enormous, and yet she was attractive and much sought after, her freshness was so pleasant. Her face was like a ruddy apple — a peony rose just burst into bloom — and out of it gazed a pair of magnificent dark eyes overshadowed by long thick lashes that deepened their blackness; and lower down, a charming little mouth, dewy to the kiss, and furnished with a row of tiny milk-white teeth. Over and above all this she was, they said, full of inestimable qualities.

No sooner was her identity recognized than a whisper ran through the ladies in which the words "prostitute" and "public scandal," were so conspicuously distinct that she raised her head and retaliated by sweeping her companions with such a bold and defiant look that deep silence instantly fell upon them, and they all cast down their eyes with the exception of Loiseau, who watched her with a kindling eye.

However, conversation was soon resumed between the three ladies, whom the presence of this "person." had suddenly rendered friendly — almost intimate. It seemed to them that they must, as it were, raise a rampart of their dignity as spouses between them and this shameless creature who made a traffic of herself; for legalized love always takes a high hand with her unlicensed sister.

The three men too, drawn to one another by a conservative instinct at sight of Cornudet, talked money in a certain tone of contempt for the impecunious. Count Hubert spoke of the damage inflicted on him by the Prussians, of the losses which would result to him from the seizing of cattle and from ruined crops, but with all the assurance of a great landed proprietor, ten times millionaire, whom these ravages might inconvenience for the space of a year at most. Monsieur Carré-Lamadon, of great experience in the cotton industry, had taken the precaution to send six hundred thousand francs across to England as provision against a rainy day. As for Loiseau, he made arrangements to sell all the common wines in his cellars to the French commission of supplies, consequently the Government owed him a formidable sum, which he counted upon receiving at Havre.

The three exchanged rapid and amicable glances. Although differing in position they felt themselves brothers in money, and of the great freemasonry of those who possess, of those who can make the gold jingle when they put their hands in the breeches-pockets.

The diligence went so slowly that by ten o'clock in the morning they had not made four leagues. The men got out three times and climbed the hill on foot. They began to grow anxious, for they were to have lunched at Tôtes, and now they despaired of reaching that place before night. Everybody was on the look-out for some inn by the way, when the vehicle stuck fast in a snow-drift, and it took two hours to get it out.

Meanwhile the pangs of hunger began to affect them severely both in mind and body, and yet not an inn, not a tavern even, was to be seen; the approach of the Prussians and the passage of the famished French troops had frightened away all trade.

The gentlemen foraged diligently for the provisions in the farms by the roadside; but they failed to obtain so much as a piece of bread, for the mistrustful peasant hid all reserve stores for fear of being pillaged by the soldiers, who, having no food supplied to them, took by force everything they could lay their hands on.

Towards one o'clock Loiseau announced that he felt a very decided void in his stomach. Everybody had been suffering in the same manner for a long time, and the violent longing for food had extinguished conversation.

From time to time some one would yawn, to be almost immediately imitated by another and then each of the rest in turn, and according to their disposition, manners, or social standing, would open their mouth noisily, or modestly cover with the hand the gaping cavity from which the breath issued in a vapour.

Boule de Suif had several times stooped down as if feeling for something under her skirts. She hesitated a moment, looked at her companions, and then composedly resumed her former position. The faces were pale and drawn. Loiseau declared he would give a thousand francs for a ham. His wife made a faint movement as to protest, but restrained herself. It always affected her painfully to hear of money being thrown away, nor could she even understand a joke upon the subject.

"To tell the truth," said the Count, "I do not feel quite myself either — how could I have omitted to think of bringing provisions?" And everybody reproached themselves with the same neglectfulness.

Cornudet, however, had a flask of rum which he offered round. It was coldly refused. Loiseau alone accepted a mouthful, and handed back the flask with thanks saying, "That's good! that warms you up and keeps the hunger off a bit." The alcohol raised his spirits somewhat, and he proposed that they should do the same as on the little ship in the song — eat the fattest of the passengers. This indirect but obvious allusion to Boule de Suif shocked the gentle people. Nobody responded and only Cornudet smiled. The two Sisters of Mercy had ceased to tell their beads and sat motionless, their hands buried in their wide sleeves, their eyes obstinately lowered, doubtless engaged in offering back to Heaven the sacrifice of suffering which it sent them.

At last, at three o'clock, when they were in the middle of an interminable stretch of bare country without a single village in sight, Boule de Suif, stooping hurriedly, drew from under the seat a large basket covered with a white napkin.

Out of it she took, first of all, a little china plate and a delicate silver drinking-cup, and then an immense dish, in which two whole fowls ready carved lay stiffened in their jelly. Other good things were visible in the basket: patties, fruits, pastry — in fact provisions for a three days' journey in order to be independent of inn cookery. The necks of four bottles protruded from between the parcels of food. She took the wing of a fowl and began to eat it daintily with one of those little rolls which they call "Regence" in Normandy.

Every eye was fixed upon her. As the odour of the food spread through the carriage nostrils began to quiver and mouths to fill with water, while the jaws, just below the ears, contracted painfully. The dislike entertained by the ladies for this abandoned young woman grew savage, almost to the point of longing to murder her or at least to turn her out into the snow, her and her drinking-cup and her basket and her provisions.

Loiseau, however, was devouring the dish of chicken with his eyes. "Madame has been more prudent than we," he said. "Some people always think of everything."

She turned her head in his direction. "If you would care for any, Monsieur — ? It is not comfortable to fast for so long."

He bowed. "By Jove! — frankly, I won't refuse. I can't stand this any longer — the fortune of war, is it not, madame?" And with a comprehensive look he added: "In moments such as this we are only too glad to find any one who will oblige us." He had a newspaper which he spread on his knee to save his trousers, and with the point of a knife which he always carried in his pocket he captured a drumstick all glazed with jelly, tore it with his teeth, and then proceeded to chew it with satisfaction so evident that a deep groan of distress went up from the whole party.

Upon this Boule de Suif in a gentle and humble tone invited the two Sisters to share the collation. They both accepted on the spot, and without raising their eyes began to eat very hurriedly, after stammering a few words of thanks. Nor did Cornudet refuse his neighbour's offer, and with the Sisters they formed a kind of table by spreading out newspapers on their knees.

The jaws opened and shut without a pause, biting, chewing, gulping ferociously. Loiseau, hard at work in his corner, urged his wife in a low voice to follow his example. She resisted for some time, then, after a pang which gripped her very vitals, she gave in. Whereupon her husband, rounding off his phrases, asked if their "charming fellow-traveller" would permit him to offer a little something to Madame Loiseau.

"Why, yes, certainly, Monsieur," she answered

with a pleasant smile, and handed him the dish.

There was a moment of embarrassment when the first bottle of claret was uncorked — there was but the one drinking-cup. Each one wiped it before passing it to the rest. Cornudet alone, from an impulse of gallantry no doubt, placed his lips on the spot still wet from the lips of his neighbour.

Then it was that, surrounded by people who were eating, suffocated by the fragrant odour of the viands, the Count and Countess de Bréville and Monsieur and Madame Carré-Lamadon suffered the agonies of that torture which has ever been associated with the name of Tantalus. Suddenly the young wife of the cotton manufacturer gave a deep sigh. Every head turned towards her; she was as white as the snow outside, her eyes closed, her head fell forward — she had fainted. Her husband, distraught with fear, implored assistance of the whole company. All lost their heads till the elder of the two Sisters, who supported the unconscious lady, forced Boule de Suif's drinking-cup between her lips and made her swallow a few drops of wine. The pretty creature stirred, opened her eyes, smiled and then declared in an expiring voice that she felt quite well now. But to prevent her being overcome again in the same manner, the Sister induced her to drink a full cup of wine, adding, "It is simply hunger — nothing else."

At this Boule de Suif, blushing violently, looked at the four starving passengers and faltered shyly, "*Mon Dieu!* If I might make so bold as to offer the ladies and gentlemen —" She stopped short, fearing a rude rebuff.

Loiseau, however, at once threw himself into the breach. "*Parbleu!* under such circumstances we are all companions in misfortune and bound to help each other. Come, ladies, don't stand on ceremony — take what you can get and be thankful: who knows whether we shall be able to find so much as a house where we can spend the night? At this rate we shall not reach Tôtes till to-morrow afternoon."

They still hesitated, nobody having the courage to take upon themselves the responsibility of the decisive "Yes." Finally the Count seized the bull by the horns. Adopting his most grandiose air, he turned with a bow to the embarrassed young woman and said, "We accept your offer with thanks, madame."

The first step only was difficult. The Rubicon once crossed, they fell to with a will. They emptied the basket, which contained, besides the provisions already mentioned: a pâté de foie gras, a lark pie, a piece of smoked tongue, some pears, a slab of gingerbread, mixed biscuits, and a cup of pickled onions and gherkins in vinegar — for, like all women, Boule de Suif adored pickles.

They could not well eat the young woman's provisions and not speak to her, so they conversed — stiffly at first, and then, seeing that she showed no signs of presuming, with less reserve. Mesdames de Bréville and Carré-Lamadon, having a great deal of *savoir vivre*, knew how to make themselves agreeable with tact and delicacy. The Countess, in particular, exhibited the amiable condescension of the extremely high-born lady whom no contact can sully, and was charming. But big Madame Loiseau, who had the soul of a gendarme, remained unmoved, speaking little and eating much.

The conversation naturally turned upon the war. They related horrible deeds committed by the Prussians and examples of the bravery of the French; all these people who were flying rendering full homage to the courage of those who remained behind. Incidents of personal experience soon followed, and Boule de Suif told, with that warmth of colouring which women of her type often employ in expressing their natural feelings, how she had come to leave Rouen.

"I thought at first I should be able to hold out," she said, "for I had plenty of provisions in my house, and would much rather feed a few soldiers than turn out of my home and go goodness knows where. But when I saw them — these Prussians — it was too much for me. They made my blood boil with rage, and I cried the whole day for shame. Oh, if I had only been a man! — well, there! I watched them from my window — fat pigs that they were with their spiked helmets — and my servant had to hold my hands to prevent me throwing the furniture down on the top of them. Then some of them came to be quartered on me, and I flew at the throat of the first one — they are not harder to strangle than any one else — and would have finished him too if they had not dragged me off by the hair. Of course I had to lie low after that. So as soon as I found an opportunity I left — and here I am."

Everybody congratulated her. She rose considerably in the estimation of her companions, who had not shown themselves of such valiant mettle, and listening to her tale, Cornudet smiled the benignant and approving smile of an apostle — as a priest might on hearing a devout person praise the Almighty; democrats with long beards having the monopoly of patriotism as the men of the cassock possess that of religion. He then took up the parable in a didactic tone with the phraseology culled from the notices posted each day on the walls, and finished up with a flourish of eloquence in which he scathingly alluded to "that blackguard Badinguet."[1]

But Boule de Suif fired up at this for she was a Bonapartist. She turned upon him with scarlet cheeks and stammering with indignation, "Ah! I should just like to have seen any of you in his place! A nice mess you would have made of it! It is men of your sort that ruined him, poor man. There would be nothing for it but to leave France for good if we were governed by cowards like you!"

Cornudet, nothing daunted, preserved a disdainful and superior smile, but there was a feeling in the air that high words would soon follow, whereupon the Count interposed, and managed, not without difficulty, to quiet the infuriated young woman by asserting authoritatively that every sincere opinion was to be respected. Nevertheless the Countess and the manufacturer's wife, who nourished in their hearts the unreasoning hatred of all well-bred people for the Republic and at the same time that instinctive weakness of all women for uniformed and

[1] Nickname for Napoleon III.

despotic governments, felt drawn, in spite of themselves, to this woman of the street who had so much sense of the fitness of things and whose opinions so closely resembled their own.

The basket was empty — this had not been difficult among ten of them — they only regretted it was not larger. The conversation was kept up for some little time longer, although somewhat more coldly after they had finished eating.

The night fell, the darkness grew gradually more profound, and the cold, to which digestion rendered them more sensitive, made even Boule de Suif shiver in spite of her fat. Madame de Bréville thereupon offered her her charcoal foot-warmer, which had been replenished several times since the morning; she accepted with alacrity, for her feet were like ice. Mesdames Carré-Lamadon and Loiseau lent theirs to the two Sisters.

The driver had lit his lanterns, which shed a vivid light over the cloud of vapour that hung over the steaming backs of the horses and over the snow at each side of the road, which seemed to open out under the shifting reflection of the lights.

Inside the conveyance nothing could be distinguished any longer, but there was a sudden movement between Boule de Suif and Cornudet, and Loiseau, peering through the gloom, fancied he saw the man with the beard start back quickly as if he had received a well-directed but noiseless blow.

Tiny points of fire appeared upon the road in front. It was Tôtes. The travellers had been driving for eleven hours, which, with the four half-hours for food and rest to the horses, made thirteen. They entered the town and stopped in front of the Hôtel du Commerce.

The door opened. A familiar sound caused every passenger to tremble—it was the clink of a scabbard on the stones. At the same moment a German voice called out something.

Although the diligence had stopped, nobody attempted to get out, as though they expected to be massacred on setting foot to the ground. The driver then appeared holding up one of the lanterns, which suddenly illumined the vehicle to its farthest corner and revealed the two rows of bewildered faces with their open mouths and startled eyes wide with alarm.

Beside the driver in the full glare of the light stood a German officer, a tall young man excessively slender and blonde, compressed into his uniform like a girl in her stays, and wearing, well over one ear, a flat black wax-cloth cap like the "Boots" of an English hotel. His preposterously long moustache, which was drawn out stiff and straight, and tapered away indefinitely to each side till it finished off in a single thread so thin that it was impossible to say where it ended, seemed to weigh upon the corners of his mouth and form a deep furrow in either cheek.

In Alsatian-French and stern accents he invited the passengers to descend: "Vill you get out, chentlemen and laties?"

The two Sisters were the first to obey with the docility of holy women accustomed to unfaltering submission. The Count and Countess appeared next, followed by the manufacturer and his wife, and after them Loiseau pushing his better half in front of him. As he set foot to the ground he remarked to the officer, more from motives of prudence than politeness, "Good evening, Monsieur," to which the other with the insolence of the man in possession, vouchsafed no reply but a stare.

Boule de Suif and Cornudet, though the nearest the door, were the last to emerge — grave and haughty in face of the enemy. The buxom young woman struggled hard to command herself and be calm; the democrat tugged at his long rusty beard with a tragic and slightly trembling hand. They sought to preserve their dignity, realizing that in such encounters each one, to a certain extent, represents his country; and the two being similarly disgusted at the servile readiness of their companions, she endeavored to show herself prouder than her fellow travellers who were honest women, while he, feeling that he must set an example, continued in his attitude his mission of resistance begun by digging pitfalls in the high roads.

They all entered the huge kitchen of the inn, and the German, having been presented with the passport signed by the general in command — where each traveller's name was accompanied by a personal description and a statement as to his or her profession — he proceeded to scrutinize the party for a long time, comparing the persons with the written notices.

Finally, he exclaimed unceremoniously, "That's all right," and disappeared.

They breathed again more freely. Hunger having reasserted itself, supper was ordered. It would take half an hour to prepare, so while two servants were apparently busied about it the travellers dispersed to look at their rooms. These were all together down each side of a long passage ending in a door marked "Toilet."

At last, just as they were sitting down to table, the innkeeper himself appeared. He was a former horsedealer, a stout asthmatic man with perpetual wheezings and blowings and rattlings of phlegm in his throat. His father had transmitted to him the name of Follenvie.

"Mademoiselle Elizabeth Rousset?" he said.

Boule de Suif started and turned round. "That is my name."

"Mademoiselle, the Prussian officer wants to speak to you at once."

"To me?"

"Yes, if you really are Mademoiselle Elizabeth Rousset."

She hesitated, thought for a moment, and then declared roundly: "That may be, but I'm not going."

There was a movement round about her — everybody was much exercised as to the reason of this summons. The Count came over to her.

"You may do wrong to refuse, madame, for it may entail considerable annoyance not only on yourself but on the rest of your companions. It is a fatal mistake ever to offer resistance to people who are stronger than ourselves. The step can have no possible danger for you — it is probably about some little formality that has been omitted."

One and all concurred with him, implored and urged and scolded, till they ended by convincing her; for they were all apprehensive of the results of her obstinacy.

"Well, it is only for your sakes that I am doing it!" she said at last. The Countess pressed her hand. "And we are most grateful to you."

She left the room, and the others agreed to wait for her before beginning the meal. Each one lamented at not having been asked for instead of this hot-headed, violent young woman, and mentally prepared any number of platitudes for the event of being called in their turn.

At the end of ten minutes she returned, crimson with rage, choking, snorting, — "Oh, the blackguard; the low blackguard!" she stammered.

They all crowded round her to know what had happened, but she would not say, and the Count becoming insistent, she answered with much dignity, "No, it does not concern anybody! I can't speak of it."

They then seated themselves round a great soup tureen from which steamed a smell of cabbage. In spite of this little contretemps the supper was a gay one. The cider, of which the Loiseaus and the two nuns partook from motives of economy, was good. The rest ordered wine and Cornudet called for beer. He had a particular way of uncorking the bottle, of making the liquid froth, of gazing at it while he tilted the glass, which he then held up between his eye and the light to enjoy the color; while he drank, his great beard, which had the tints of his favourite beverage, seemed to quiver fondly, his eyes squinting that he might not lose sight of his tankard for a moment, and altogether he had the appearance of fulfilling the sole function for which he had been born. You would have said that he established in his own mind some connection or affinity between the two great passions that monopolized his life — Ale and Revolution — and most assuredly he never tasted the one without thinking of the other.

Monsieur and Madame Follenvie dined at the farther end of the table. The husband — puffing and blowing like an exploded locomotive — had too much cold on the chest to be able to speak and eat at the same time, but his wife never ceased talking. She described her every impression at the arrival of the Prussians and all they did and all they said, execrating them in the first place because they cost so much, and secondly because she had two sons in the army. She addressed herself chiefly to the Countess, as it flattered her to be able to say she had conversed with a lady of quality.

She presently lowered her voice and proceeded to recount some rather delicate matters, her husband breaking in from time to time with — "You had much better hold your tongue, Madame Follenvie," — to which she paid not the slightest attention, but went on.

"Well, madame, as I was saying — these men, they do nothing but eat potatoes and pork and pork and potatoes from morning till night. And as for their habits — ! Saving your presence, they make dirt everywhere. And you should see them exercising for hours and days together out there in the fields — It's forward march and backward march, and turn this way and turn that. If they even worked in the fields or mended the roads in their own country! But, no, madame, these soldiers are no good to anybody, and the poor people have to keep them and feed them simply that they may learn how to murder. I know I am only a poor ignorant old woman, but when I see these men wearing themselves out by tramping up and down from morning till night, I cannot help saying to myself, if there are some people who make a lot of useful discoveries, why should others give themselves so much trouble to do harm? After all, isn't it an abomination to kill anybody, no matter whether they are Prussians, or English, or Poles, or French? If you revenge yourself on some one who has harmed you, that is wicked, for you are punished; but let them shoot down our sons as if they were game, and it is all right, and they give medals to the man who kills the most. No, no, I say, I shall never be able to see any rhyme or reason in that!"

"War is barbarous if one attacks an unoffending neighbour — it is a sacred duty if one defends one's country," remarked Cornudet in a declamatory tone.

The old woman drooped her head. "Yes — defending oneself, of course, that is quite another thing; but wouldn't it be better to kill all these kings who do this for their pleasure?"

Cornudet's eyes flashed. "Bravo, citizeness!" he cried.

Monsieur Carré-Lamadon was lost in thought.

Although he was an ardent admirer of famous military men, the sound common sense of this peasant woman made him reflect upon the wealth which would necessarily accrue to the country if all these unemployed and consequently ruinous hands — so much unproductive force — were available for the great industrial works that would take centuries to complete.

Loiseau meanwhile had left his seat and gone over beside the innkeeper, to whom he began talking in a low voice. The fat man laughed, coughed, and spat, his unwieldy stomach shaking with mirth at his neighbour's jokes, and he bought six hogsheads of claret from him for the spring when the Prussians would have cleared out.

Supper was scarcely over when, dropping with fatigue, everybody went off to bed.

Loiseau, however, who had noticed certain things, let his wife go to bed and proceeded to glue first his ear and then his eye to the keyhole, endeavouring to penetrate what he called "the mysteries of the corridor."

After about an hour he heard a rustling, and hurrying to the keyhole, he perceived Boule de Suif looking ampler than ever in a dressing-gown of blue cashmere trimmed with white lace. She had a candle in her hand and was going towards the door at the end of the corridor. Then a door at one side opened cautiously, and when she returned after a few minutes, Cornudet in his shirt-sleeves was following her. They were talking in a low voice and presently stood still; Boule de Suif apparently defending the entrance of her room with much energy. Unfortunately Loiseau was unable to hear what they said, but at last, as they raised their voices somewhat, he caught a word or two. Cornudet was insisting eagerly. "Look here," he said, "you are really very ridiculous — what difference can it make to you?"

And she with an offended air retorted, "No! — let me tell you there are moments when that sort of thing won't do; and besides — here — it would be a crying shame."

He obviously did not understand. "Why?"

At this she grew angry. "Why?" and she raised her voice still more, "you don't see why? and there are Prussians in the house — in the next room for all you know!"

He made no reply. This display of patriotic prudery evidently aroused his failing dignity, for with a brief kiss he made for his own door on tiptoe.

Loiseau, deeply thrilled and amused, executed a double shuffle in the middle of the room, donned his nightcap, slipped into the blankets where the bony figure of his spouse already reposed, and waking her with a kiss he murmured: "Do you love me, darling?"

The whole house sank to silence. But anon there arose from somewhere — it might have been the cellar, it might have been the attics — impossible to determine the direction — a rumbling — sonorous, even, regular, dull, prolonged roar as of a boiler under high steam pressure: Monsieur Follenvie slept.

It had been decided that they should start at eight o'clock the next morning, so they were all assembled in the kitchen by that hour; but the diligence, roofed with snow, stood solitary in the middle of the courtyard without horses or driver. The latter was sought for in vain either in the stables or in the coachhouse. The men of the party then resolved to beat the country round for him, and went out accordingly. They found themselves in the public square with the church at one end, and low-roofed houses down each side in which they caught sight of Prussian soldiers. The first one they came upon was peeling potatoes; farther on another was washing out a barber's shop; while a third, bearded to the eyes, was soothing a crying child and rocking it to and fro on his knee to quiet it. The big peasant women whose men were all "with the army in the war" were ordering about their docile conquerors and showing them by signs what work they wanted done — chopping wood, grinding coffee, fetching water; one of them was even doing the washing for his hostess, a helpless old crone.

The Count, much astonished, stopped the beadle, who happened to come out of the priest's house at that moment, and asked the meaning of it all.

"Oh," replied the old church rat, "these are not at all bad. From what I hear they are not Prussians, either; they come from farther off, but where I can't say; and they have all left a wife and children at home. I am very sure the women down there are crying for their men, too, and it will all make a nice lot of misery for them as well as for us. We are not so badly off here for the moment, because they do no harm and are working just as if they were in their own homes. You see, Monsieur, the poor always help one another; it is the bigwigs who make the wars."

Cornudet, indignant at the friendly understanding established between the victors and the vanquished, retired from the scene, preferring to shut himself up in the inn. Loiseau of course must have his joke. "They are re-populating," he said. Monsieur Carré-Lamadon found a more fitting expression. "They are making reparations."

But the driver was nowhere to be found. At last he was unearthed in the village café hobnobbing fraternally with the officer's orderly.

"Did you not have orders to have the diligence ready by eight o'clock?" the Count asked him.

"Oh, yes, but I got another order later on."

"What?"

"Not to put the horses in at all."

"Who gave you that order?"

"Why, — the Prussian commandant."

"Why?"

"I don't know — you had better ask him. I am told not to harness the horses, and so I don't harness them — there you are."

"Did he tell you so himself?"

"No, Monsieur, the innkeeper brought me the message from him."

"When was that?"

"Last night, just as I was going to bed."

The three men returned much disconcerted. They asked for Monsieur Follenvie, but were informed by the servant that on account of his asthma he never got up before ten o'clock — he had even positively forbidden them to awaken him before then except in case of fire.

Then they asked to see the officer, but that was absolutely impossible, although he lodged at the inn.

Monsieur Follenvie alone was authorized to approach him on non-military matters. So they had to wait. The women returned to their rooms and occupied themselves as best they could.

Cornudet installed himself in the high chimney-corner of the kitchen, where a great fire was burning. He had one of the little coffee-room tables brought to him and a can of beer, and puffed away placidly at his pipe, which enjoyed among the democrats almost equal consideration with himself, as if in serving Cornudet it served the country also. The pipe was a superb meerschaum, admirably coloured, black as the teeth of its owner, but fragrant, curved, shining familiar to his hand, and the natural complement to his physiognomy. He sat there motionless, his eyes fixed alternately on the flame of the hearth and the foam on the top of his tankard, and each time after drinking he passed his bony fingers with a self-satisfied gesture through his long greasy hair, while he absorbed the fringe of froth from his moustache.

Under the pretext of stretching his legs, Loiseau went out and palmed off his wines on the country retail dealers. The Count and the manufacturer talked politics. They forecast the future of France, the one putting his faith in the Orleans, the other in an unknown saviour, a hero who would come to the fore when things were at their very worst —

a Du Guesclin, a Joan of Arc perhaps, or even another Napoleon I. Ah, if only the Prince Imperial were not so young! Cornudet listened to them with the smile of a man who could solve the riddle of Fate if he would. His pipe perfumed the whole kitchen with its balmy fragrance.

On the stroke of ten Monsieur Follenvie made his appearance. They instantly attacked him with questions, but he had but one answer which he repeated two or three times without variation. "The officer said to me, 'Monsieur Follenvie, you will forbid them to harness the horses for these travellers to-morrow morning. They are not to leave till I give my permission. You understand?' That is all."

They demanded to see the officer; the Count sent up his card, on which Monsieur Carré-Lamadon added his name and all his titles. The Prussian sent word that he would admit the two men to his presence after he had lunched, that is to say, about one o'clock.

The ladies came down and they all managed to eat a little in spite of their anxiety. Boule de Suif looked quite ill and very much agitated.

They were just finishing coffee when the orderly arrived to fetch the two gentlemen.

Loiseau joined them, but when they proposed to bring Cornudet along to give more solemnity to their proceedings, he declared haughtily that nothing would induce him to enter into any communication whatsoever with the Germans, and he returned to his chimney-corner and ordered another bottle of beer.

The three men went upstairs, and were shown into the best room in the inn, where they were received by the officer lolling in an arm-chair, his heels on the chimney-piece, smoking a long porcelain pipe, and arrayed in a flamboyant dressing-gown, taken, no doubt, from the abandoned dwelling-house of some bourgeois of inferior taste. He did not rise, he vouchsafed them no greeting of any description, he did not even look at them — a brilliant sample of the victorious military cad.

At last after some moments, waiting he said: "Vat do you vant?"

The Count acted as spokesman.

"We wish to leave, Monsieur."

"No."

"May I take the liberty of asking the reason for this refusal?"

"Pecause I do not shoose."

"With all due respect, Monsieur, I would draw your attention to the fact that your general gave us a permit for Dieppe, and I cannot see that we have done anything to justify your hard measures."

"I do not shoose — dat's all — you can co town."

They all bowed and withdrew.

The afternoon was miserable. They could make nothing of this caprice of the German's, and the most far-fetched ideas tortured their minds. The whole party remained in the kitchen engaging in endless discussions, imagining the most improbable things. Were they to be kept as hostages? — but if so, to what end? — or taken prisoners — or asked a large ransom? This last suggestion threw them into a cold perspiration of fear. The wealthiest were seized with the worst panic and saw themselves forced, if they valued their lives, to empty bags of gold into the rapacious hands of this soldier. They racked their brains for plausible lies to dissemble their riches, to pass themselves off as poor — very poor. Loiseau pulled off his watch-chain and hid it in his pocket. As night fell their apprehensions increased. The lamp was lighted, and as there were still two hours till supper Madame Loiseau proposed a game of thirty-one. It would be some little distraction, at any rate. The plan was accepted; even Cornudet, who had put out his pipe from motives of politeness, taking a hand.

The Count shuffled the cards, dealt, Boule de Suif had thirty-one at the first deal; and very soon the interest in the game allayed the fears that beset their minds. Cornudet, however, observed that the two Loiseaus were in league to cheat.

Just as they were sitting down to the evening meal Monsieur appeared and said in his husky voice: "The Prussian officer wishes to know if Mademoiselle Elizabeth Rousset has not changed her mind yet?"

Boule de Suif remained standing and turned very pale, then suddenly her face flamed and she fell into such a paroxysm of rage that she could not speak. At last she burst out: "You can tell that scoundrel — that low scum of a Prussian — that I won't — and I never will — do you hear? — never! never! never!"

The fat innkeeper retired. They instantly surrounded Boule de Suif, questioning, entreating her to disclose the mystery of her visit. At first she refused, but presently she was carried away by her indignation: "What does he want? — what does he want? — he wants me to make love to him!" she shouted.

The general indignation was so violent that nobody was shocked. Cornudet brought his beer glass down on the table with such a bang that it broke. There was a perfect babel of invective against the drunken lout, a hurricane of wrath, a union of all for resistance, as if each had been required to contribute a portion of the sacrifice demanded of her. The Count protested with disgust that these people behaved really as if they were early barbarians. The women, in particular, accorded her the most lively and affectionate sympathy. The nuns, who only appeared at meals, dropped their eyes and said nothing.

The first fury of the storm having abated, they sat down to supper, but there was little conversation and a good deal of thoughtful abstraction.

The ladies retired early; the men, while they smoked, got up a game of écarté, which Monsieur Follenvie was invited to join, as they intended pumping him skilfully as to the means that could be employed for overcoming the officer's opposition to their departure. Unfortunately, he would absorb himself wholly in his cards, and neither listened to what they said nor gave any answer to their questions, but repeated incessantly, "Play, gentlemen, play!" His attention was so deeply engaged that he forgot to spit, which caused his chest to wheeze from time to time; his wheezing lungs running through the whole gamut of asthma from notes of the profoundest bass to the shrill, hoarse crow of the young cock.

He refused to go to bed when his wife, who was dropping with sleep, came to fetch him. She therefore departed alone, for on her devolved the "day duty," and she always rose with the sun, while her husband took the "night duty," and was always ready to sit up all night with friends. He merely called out, "Mind you put my egg flip in front of the fire!" and returned to his cards. When they were convinced that there was nothing to be got out of him, they declared that it was high time to go to bed, and left him.

They were up again pretty early the next day, filled with an indefinite hope, a still keener desire to be gone, and a horror of another day to be got through in this horrible little inn.

Alas! the horses were still in the stable and the coachman remained invisible. For lack of something better to do, they sadly wandered round the diligence.

Lunch was very depressing, and a certain chilliness had sprung up with regard to Boule de Suif, for the night—which brings counsel—had somewhat modified their opinions. They were almost vexed with the girl now for not having gone to the Prussian secretly, and thus prepared a pleasant surprise for her companions in the morning. What could be simpler, and, after all, who could have been any the wiser? She might have saved appearances by telling the officer that she could not bear to see their distress any longer. It could make so very little difference to her one way or another!

But, as yet, nobody confessed to these thoughts.

In the afternoon, as they were feeling bored to extinction, the Count proposed a walk round the village. Everybody wrapped up carefully and the little party started, with the exception of Cornudet, who preferred sitting by the fire, and the two Sisters, who passed their days in the church or with the curé.

The cold — grown more intense each day — nipped their noses and ears viciously, and the feet became so painful that every step was anguish; but when they caught sight of the open stretch of country it appeared to them so appallingly lugubrious under its illimitable white covering that they turned back with one accord, their hearts constricted, their spirits below zero. The four ladies walked in front, the three men following a little behind.

Loiseau, who thoroughly took in the situation, suddenly broke out, "How long was this damned wench going to keep them hanging on in this hole?" The Count, courteous as ever, observed that one could not demand so painful a sacrifice of any woman — the offer must come from her. Monsieur Carré-Lamadon remarked that if — as there was every reason to believe — the French made an offensive counter-march by way of Dieppe, the collision could only take place at Tôtes. This reflection greatly alarmed the other two. "Why not escape on foot?" suggested Loiseau. The Count shrugged his shoulders. "How can you think of such a thing in this snow — and with our wives? Besides which, we should instantly be pursued, caught in ten minutes, and brought back prisoners at the mercy of these soldiers." This was incontestable — there was nothing more to be said.

The ladies talked dress, but a certain constraint seemed to have risen up between them.

All at once, at the end of the street, the officer came in sight, his tall figure, like a wasp in uniform, silhouetted against the dazzling background of snow, and walking with his knees well apart, with that movement peculiar to the military when endeavouring to save their carefully polished boots from the mud.

In passing the ladies he bowed, but only stared contemptuously at the men, who, be it said, had the dignity not to lift their hats, though Loiseau made a faint gesture in that direction.

Boule de Suif blushed up to her eyes, and the three married women felt it a deep humiliation to have encountered this soldier while they were in the company of the young woman he had treated so cavalierly.

The conversation then turned upon him, his general appearance, his face. Madame Carré-Lamadon, who had known a great many officers and was competent to judge of them as a connoisseur, considered this one really not half bad — she even regretted that he was not French, he would have made such a fascinating hussar, and would certainly have been much run after.

Once indoors again, they did not know what to do with themselves. Sharp words were exchanged on the most insignificant pretexts. The silent dinner did not last long, and they shortly afterwards went to bed, hoping to kill time by sleeping.

They came down next morning with jaded faces and exasperation in their hearts. The women scarcely addressed a word to Boule de Suif.

Presently the church bell began to ring; it was for a christening. Boule de Suif had a child out at nurse with some peasants near Yvetot. She did not see it once in a year and never gave it a thought, but the idea of this baby which was going to be baptized filled her heart with sudden and violent tenderness for her own, and nothing would satisfy her but that she should assist at the ceremony.

No sooner was she gone than they all looked at one another and proceeded to draw up their chairs; for everybody felt that things had come to that point that something must be decided upon. Loiseau had an inspiration: that they should propose to the officer to keep Boule de Suif and let the rest go.

Monsieur Follenvie undertook the mission, but returned almost immediately. The German, who had some knowledge of human nature, had simply turned him out of the room. He meant to retain the whole party so long as his desire was unsatisfied.

At this Madame Loiseau's plebeian tendencies got the better of her. "But surely we are not going to sit down calmly here and die of old age! As that is this harlot's trade, I don't see that she has any right to refuse one man more than another. Why, she took anybody she could get in Rouen, down to the very cab drivers. Yes, Madame, the coachman of the Prefecture. I know all about it. He buys his wine at our shop. And now, when it lies with her to get us out of this scrape, she pretends to be particular — the brazen hussy! For my part, I consider the officer has behaved very well! He has probably not had a chance for some time, and there were three here whom, no doubt, he would have preferred; but no — he is content to take the one who is public property. He respects married women. Remember, he is master here. He had only to say 'I will,' and he could have taken us by force with his soldiers!"

A little shudder ran through the other two women. Pretty little Madame Carré-Lamadon's eyes shone and she turned rather pale as though she already felt herself forcibly seized by the officer.

The men, who had been arguing the matter in a corner, now joined them. Loiseau, foaming with rage, was for delivering up "the hussy" bound hand and foot to the enemy. But the Count, coming of three generations of ambassadors, and gifted with the physique of the diplomatist, was on the side of skill as opposed to brute force.

"She must be persuaded," he said. Whereupon they conspired.

The women drew up closer together, voices were lowered, and the discussion became general, each one offering his or her advice. Nothing was said to shock the proprieties. The ladies, in particular, were most expert in felicitous turns of phrase, charming subtleties of speech for expressing the most ticklish things. A foreigner would have understood nothing, the language was so carefully veiled. But as the slight coating of modesty with which every woman of the world is enveloped is hardly more than skin deep, they expanded under the influence of this equivocal adventure, enjoying themselves tremendously at bottom, thoroughly in their element, dabbling in sensuality with the gusto of an epicurean cook preparing a toothsome delicacy for somebody else.

The story finally appeared to them so funny that they quite recovered their spirits. The Count indulged in some rather risky pleasantries, but so well put that they raised a responsive smile; Loiseau, in his turn, rapped out some decidedly strong jokes which nobody took in bad part, and the brutal proposition expressed by his wife swayed all their minds: "As that is her trade, why refuse one man more than another?" Little Madame Carré-Lamadon seemed even to think that in her place she would refuse this one less readily than another.

They were long in preparing the blockade, as if against an invested fortress. Each one agreed upon the part they would play, the arguments they would bring forward, the manœuvres they would execute. They arranged the plan of attack, the stratagems to be employed, and the surprises of the assault for forcing this living citadel to receive the enemy within its gates. Cornudet alone held aloof, completely outside the affair.

They were so profoundly occupied with the matter in hand that they never heard Boule de Suif enter the room. But the Count breathed a low warning "Hush!" and they lifted their heads. She was there. The talking ceased abruptly, and a certain feeling of embarrassment prevented them from addressing her at first, till the Countess, more versed than the others in the duplicities of the drawing-room, asked how she had enjoyed the christening.

Still full of emotion at what she had witnessed, Boule de Suif described every detail — the peoples' faces, their attitudes, even the appearance of the church. It was so nice to pray now and then, she added.

Till luncheon, however, the ladies confined themselves merely to being agreeable to her in order to increase her confidence in them and her docility to their counsels. But once seated at the table, the attack began. It first took the form of a desultory conversation on devotion to a cause. Examples from ancient history were cited: Judith and Holofernes, and then, without any apparent connection, Lucretia and Sextus, Cleopatra admitting to her couch all the hostile generals, and reducing them to the servility of slaves. Then began a fantastic history, which had sprung up in the minds of the ignorant millionaires, in which the women of Rome were seen on their way to Capua, to rock Hannibal to sleep in their arms, and his officers along with him, and the phalanxes of the mercenaries. The women were mentioned who had arrested the course of conquerors, made of their bodies a rampart, a means of dominating, a weapon; who had vanquished by their heroic embraces beings hideous or repulsive, and sacrificed their chastity to vengeance or patriotism. They even talked in veiled terms of an Englishwoman of good family who had herself inoculated with a horrible contagious disease, in order to give it to Napoleon, who was saved miraculously by a sudden indisposition at the hour of the fatal meeting.

And all this in so discreet and moderate a manner,

with now and then a little burst of warm enthusiasm, admirably calculated to excite emulation. To hear them you would have finally come to the conclusion that woman's sole mission here below was to perpetually sacrifice her person, to abandon herself continually to the caprices of the warrior.

The two Sisters appeared to be deaf to it all, sunk in profound thought. Boule de Suif said nothing.

They allowed her all the afternoon for reflection, but instead of calling her "Madame," as they had done up till now, they addressed her simply as "Mademoiselle" — nobody could have said exactly why — as if to send her down a step in the esteem she had gained, and force her to feel the shame of her position.

In the evening just as the soup was being brought to the table Monsieur Follenvie made his appearance again with the same message as before: "The Prussian officer sends to ask Mademoiselle Elizabeth Rousset if she had not changed her mind."

"No, Monsieur," Boule de Suif replied curtly.

At supper the coalition weakened. Loiseau put his foot in it three times. They all racked their brains for fresh instances to the point, and found none, when the Countess, possibly without premeditation and only from a vague desire to render homage to religion, interrogated the older of the two Sisters on the main incidents in the lives of the saints. Now, several of them had committed acts which would be counted crimes in our eyes, but the Church readily pardons such misdeeds when they are accomplished for the glory of God or the benefit of our neighbours. It was a powerful argument, and the Countess took advantage of it. Then by one of those tacit agreements, those veiled complaisances in which every one who wears ecclesiastical habit excels, or perhaps simply from a happy want of intelligence, a helpful stupidity, the old nun brought formidable support to the conspiracy. They had imagined her timid; she proved herself bold, verbose, violent. She was not troubled by any of the shilly-shallyings of casuistry, her doctrine was like a bar of iron, her faith never wavered, her conscience knew no scruples. She considered Abraham's sacrifice a very simple affair, for she herself would have instantly killed father or mother at an order from above, and nothing, she averred, could displease the Lord if the intention were commendable. The Countess, taking advantage of the sacred authority of her unexpected ally, drew her on to make an edifying paraphrase, as it were, on the well-known moral maxim: "The end justifies the means."

"Then, Sister," she inquired, "you think God approves of every pathway that leads to Him, and pardons the deed if the motive be a pure one?"

"Who can doubt it, Madame? An action blamable in itself is often rendered meritorious by the impulse which inspires it."

And she continued in the same strain, unravelling the intricacies of the will of the Almighty, predicting His decisions, making Him interest Himself in matters which, of a truth, did not concern Him at all.

All this was skillfully and discreetly wrapped up,

but each word of the pious woman in the big white cap made a breach in the indignant resistance of the courtesan. The conversation then glancing off slightly, the woman of the pendent rosaries went on to speak of the religious houses of her Order, of her superior, of herself and her fragile little companion, her dear little Sister St. Nicephora. They had been summoned to Havre to nurse the hundreds of soldiers there down with smallpox. She described the condition of these poor wretches, gave details of their disease; and while they were thus stopped upon the road by the whim of this Prussian, many French soldiers might die whom perhaps they could have saved. That was her specialty — nursing soldiers. She had been in the Crimea, in Italy, in Austria; and relating her campaigns, she suddenly revealed herself as one of those Sisters of the fife and drum who seem made for following the camp, picking up the wounded in the thick of battle, and better than any officer for quelling with a word the great hulking undisciplined louts — a regular Sister Rataplan, her ravaged face all pitted with innumerable holes, calling up an image of the devastations of war.

No one spoke after her for fear of spoiling the excellent effect.

Immediately after dinner they hurried to their rooms, not to reappear till pretty late the next morning.

Luncheon passed off quietly. They allowed the seed sown yesterday time to grow and bear fruit.

In the afternoon the Countess proposed a walk, whereupon the Count, following the preconcerted arrangement, took Boule de Suif's arm and fell behind with her a little. He adopted that familiar, paternal, somewhat contemptuous tone which elderly men affect towards such girls, calling her "my dear child," treating her from the height of his social position and indisputable respectability.

He came to the point without further preamble. "So you prefer to keep us here exposed like yourself to all the violence which must inevitably follow a check to the Prussian arms, rather than consent to accord one of those favours you have so often dispensed in your time?"

Boule de Suif did not reply.

He then appealed to her kindness of heart, her reason, her sentiment. He knew how to remain "Monsieur le Comte," yet showing himself at the same time chivalrous, flattering — in a word, altogether amiable. He exalted the sacrifice she would be making for them, touched upon their gratitude, and with a final flash of roguishness, "Besides, my dear, he may think himself lucky — he will not find many such pretty girls as you in his own country!"

Boule de Suif said nothing and rejoined the rest of the party.

When they returned, she went straight to her room and did not come down again. The anxiety was terrible. What was she going to do? How unspeakably mortifying if she still persisted in her refusal!

The dinner-hour arrived, they waited for her in vain. Monsieur Follenvie, entering presently, announced that Mademoiselle Rousset was indisposed, and that there was consequently no need to delay supper any longer. They all pricked up their ears. The Count approached the innkeeper with a whispered "All right?"

"Yes."

For propriety's sake he said nothing to his companions, but he made them a slight sign of the head. A great sigh of relief went up from every heart, every face lit up with joy.

"*Saperlipopette!*" cried Loiseau, "I will stand champagne if there is such a thing in this establishment!"

Madame Loiseau suffered a pang of anguish when the innkeeper returned with four bottles in his hands. Everybody suddenly turned communicative and cheerful, and their hearts overflowed with prurient delight. The Count seemed all at once to become aware that Madame Carré-Lamadon was charming; the manufacturer paid compliments to the Countess. Conversation became lively, sprightly, and full of sparkle.

Suddenly Loiseau, with an anxious expression, raised his arms and shouted: "Silence!" They all stopped talking, surprised and already terrified. Then he listened intently, motioning to them to be silent with his two hands, and raising his eyes to the ceiling. He listened again, and resumed in his natural voice: "It is all right. Don't worry."

They did not understand at first, but soon a smile spread over their faces.

A quarter of an hour later he began the same comedy, and repeated it frequently during the evening. He pretended to be questioning some one on the floor above, giving advice in double-meaning phrases which he drew from his repertory as a commercial traveller. At times he would assume an air of sadness, and sigh: "Poor girl;" or he would mutter between his teeth with a furious air: "You swine of a Prussian!" — Sometimes, when least expected, he would shout in resonant tones: "Enough! Enough!" adding, as though speaking to himself, "if only we see her again; if the scoundrel does not kill her!"

Although these jokes were in deplorable taste, they amused everyone and hurt nobody, for, like everything else, indignation is qualified by circumstances, and the atmosphere about them had gradually become charged with obscene thoughts.

By the time they reached dessert the women themselves were indulging in decidedly risky witticisms. Eyes grew bright, tongues were loosened, a good deal of wine had been consumed. The Count, who, even in his cups, retained his characteristic air of diplomatic gravity, made some highly spiced comparisons on the subject of the end of the winter season at the Pole and the joy of ice-bound mariners at sight of an opening to the south.

Loiseau, now in full swing, rose, and lifting high his glass of champagne, "To our deliverance!" he cried. Everybody started to their feet with acclamation. Even the two Sisters of Mercy, yielding to the solicitations of the ladies, consented to take a sip of the effervescing wine which they had never tasted before. They pronounced it to be very like lemonade, though the taste was finer.

"What a pity there is no piano," said Loiseau

as a crowning point to the situation, "we might have finished up with a quadrille."

Cornudet had not uttered a word, nor made a sign of joining in the general hilarity; he was apparently plunged in the gravest abstractions, only pulling viciously at his great beard from time to time as if to draw it out longer than before. At last, about midnight, when the company was preparing to separate, Loiseau came stumbling over to him, and digging him in the ribs: "You seem rather down in the mouth this evening, citizen — haven't said a word."

Cornudet threw up his head angrily, and sweeping the company with a flashing and terrible look: "I tell you all that what you have done to-day is infamous!"

He rose, made his way to the door, exclaimed once again, "Infamous!" and vanished.

This somewhat dashed their spirits for the moment. Loiseau, nonplussed at first, soon regained his aplomb and burst into a roar of laughter. "Sour grapes, old man — sour grapes!"

The others not understanding the allusion, he proceeded to relate the "mysteries of the corridor." This was followed by an uproarious revival of gaiety. The ladies were in a frenzy of delight, the Count and Monsieur Carré-Lamadon laughed till they cried. They could not believe it.

"Do you mean to say he wanted —"

"I tell you I saw it with my own eyes."

"And she refused?"

"Because the Prussian was in the next room."

"It is incredible."

"As true as I stand here!"

The Count nearly choked; the manufacturer held both his sides.

"And you can understand that he does not quite see the joke of the thing this evening — oh, no — not at all!"

And they all three went off again, breathless, choking, sick with laughter.

After that they parted for the night. But Madame Loiseau remarked to her husband when they were alone that that little cat of a Carré-Lamadon had laughed on the wrong side of her mouth all the evening. "You know how it is with these women — they dote upon a uniform, and whether it is French or Prussian matters precious little to them. But, Lord — it seems to me a poor way of looking at things."

All night the darkness of the corridor seemed full of thrills, of slight noises, scarcely audible, the pattering of bare feet, and creaking that was almost imperceptible. Certainly nobody got to sleep until very late, for it was long before the lights ceased to shine under the doors. Champagne, they say, often has that disturbing effect; it makes one restless and wakeful.

Next morning a brilliant winter sun shone on the dazzling snow. The diligence was by this time ready and waiting before the door, while a flock of white pigeons, muffled in their thick plumage, strutted solemnly in and out among the feet of the six horses, seeking what they might devour.

The driver, enveloped in his sheepskin, sat on the box smoking his pipe, and the radiant travellers were busily laying in provisions for the rest of the journey.

They were only waiting now for Boule de Suif. She appeared.

She looked agitated and downcast as she advanced timidly towards her fellow travellers, who all, with one movement, turned away their heads as if they had not seen her. The Count, with a dignified movement, took his wife by the arm and drew her away from this contaminating contact.

The poor thing stopped short, bewildered; then gathering up her courage she accosted the wife of the manufacturer with a humble "Good morning, Madame." The other merely replied with an impertinent little nod, accompanied by a stare of outraged virtue. Everybody seemed suddenly extremely busy, and they avoided her as if she had brought the plague in her skirts. They then precipitated themselves into the vehicle, where she arrived the last and by herself, and resumed in silence the seat she had occupied during the first part of the journey.

They affected not to see her, not to recognize her; only Madame Loiseau, glancing round at her with scorn and indignation, said half audibly to her husband, "It's a good thing that I am not sitting beside her!"

The heavy conveyance jolted off, and the journey recommenced.

No one spoke for the first little while. Boule de Suif did not venture to raise her eyes. She felt incensed at her companions, and at the same time deeply humiliated at having yielded to their persuasions, and let herself be sullied by the kisses of this Prussian into whose arms they had hypocritically thrust her.

The Countess was the first to break the uncomfortable silence. Turning to Madame Carré-Lamadon, she said, "You know Madame d'Etrelles, I think?"

"Oh, yes; she is a great friend of mine."

"What a charming woman!"

"Fascinating! So truly refined; very cultivated, too, and an artist to the tips of her fingers — she sings delightfully, and draws to perfection."

The manufacturer was talking to the Count, and through the rattle of the crazy window-panes one caught a word here and there; shares — dividends — premium — settling day — and the like. Loiseau, who had appropriated an old pack of cards from the inn, thick with the grease of the five years' rubbing on dirty tables, started a game of bezique with his wife. The two Sisters pulled up the long rosaries hanging at their waists, made the sign of the cross, and suddenly began moving their lips rapidly, faster and faster, hurrying their vague babble as if for a wager; kissing a medal from time to time, crossing themselves again, and then resuming their rapid and monotonous murmur.

Cornudet sat motionless — thinking.

At the end of the three hours' steady travelling Loiseau gathered up his cards and remarked facetiously, "It's turning hungry."

His wife then produced a parcel, which she untied, and brought out a piece of cold veal. This she cut up into thin, firm slices, and both began to eat.

"Supposing we do the same?" said the Countess, and proceeded to unpack the provisions prepared for both couples. In one of those oblong dishes with a china hare upon the cover to indicate that a roast hare lies beneath, was a succulent selection of cold viands — brown slices of juicy venison mingled with other meats. A delicious square of Gruyère cheese wrapped in newspaper still bore imprinted on its dewy surface the words "General News."

The two Sisters brought out a sausage smelling of garlic, and Cornudet, plunging his hands into the vast pockets of his loose greatcoat, drew up four hard-boiled eggs from one and a big crust of bread from the other. He peeled off the shells and threw them into the straw under his feet, and proceeded to bite into the egg, dropping pieces of the yolk into his long beard, from whence they shone out like stars.

In the hurry and confusion of the morning Boule de Suif had omitted to take thought for the future, and she looked on, furious, choking with mortification, at these people all munching away so placidly. A storm of rage convulsed her, and she opened her mouth to hurl at them the torrent of abuse that rose to her lips, but she could not speak, suffocated by her indignation.

Nobody looked at her, nobody thought of her. She felt herself drowning in the flood of contempt shown towards her by these honest scoundrels who had first sacrificed her and then cast her off like some useless and unclean thing. Then her thoughts reverted to her great basket full of good things which they had so greedily devoured — the two fowls in their glittering coat of jelly, her patties, her pears, her four bottles of claret; and her fury suddenly subsided like the breaking of an over-strung chord and she felt that she was on the verge of tears. She made the most strenuous efforts to overcome it — straightened herself up and choked back her sobs as children do, but the tears would rise. They glittered for a moment on her lashes, and presently two big drops rolled slowly over her cheeks. Others gathered in quick succession like water dripping from a rock and splashed on to the ample curve of her bosom. She sat up very straight, her eyes fixed, her face pale and rigid, hoping that nobody would notice.

But the Countess saw her and nudged her husband. He shrugged his shoulders as much as to say, "What can you expect? It is not my fault." Madame Loiseau gave a silent chuckle of triumph and murmured, "She is crying over her shame." The two Sisters had resumed their devotions after carefully wrapping up the remnants of their sausages.

Then Cornudet, while digesting his eggs, stretched his long legs under the opposite seat, leaned back, smiled like a man who has just thought of a capital joke, and began to softly whistle the *Marseillaise*.

The faces clouded; the popular air seemed unpleasing to his neighbors; they became nervous — irritable — looking as if they were ready to throw back their heads and howl like dogs at the sound of a barrel organ. He was perfectly aware of this, but did not stop. From time to time he hummed a few of the words:

Amour sacré de la patrie,
Conduis, soutiens nos bras vengeurs,
Liberté, liberté chérie,
Combats avec tes défenseurs !

They drove at a much quicker pace to-day, the snow being harder; and all the way to Dieppe, during the long, dull hours of the journey, through all the jolting and rattling of the conveyance, in the falling shades of evening and later in the profound darkness of the carriage he continued with unabated persistency his vengeful and monotonous whistling; forcing his wearied and exasperated fellow travellers to follow the song from end to end and to remember every word that corresponded to each note.

And Boule de Suif wept on, and at times a sob which she could not repress broke out between two couplets in the darkness.

MADAME TELLIER'S ESTABLISHMENT

THEY used to go there every evening at about eleven o'clock, just as they went to the café. Six or eight of them used to meet there; they were always the same set, not fast men, but respectable citizens, and young men of the town, and they used to drink their Chartreuse, and tease the girls, or else they would talk seriously with Madame, whom everybody respected, and then they used to go home before twelve o'clock. The younger men would sometimes stay the night.

It was a small, homely kind of house, painted yellow, at the corner of a street behind Saint Étienne's church, and from the windows one could see the docks, full of ships which were being unloaded, the great salt marsh, called "La Retenue," and behind, the old, gray chapel, dedicated to the Virgin, on the hill.

Madame, who came of a respectable family of peasant proprietors in the department of the Eure, had taken up that profession, just as she would have become a milliner or dressmaker. The prejudice against prostitution, which is so violent and deeply rooted in large towns, does not exist in the country places in Normandy. The peasant says: "It is a paying business," and he sends his daughter to keep a harem of fast girls, just as he would send her to keep a girls' school.

She had inherited the house from an old uncle, to whom it had belonged. Monsieur and Madame, who had formerly been innkeepers near Yvetot, had immediately sold their house, as they thought that the business at Fécamp was more profitable, and they arrived one fine morning to assume the direction of the enterprise, which was declining on account of the absence of the owners. They were good people enough in their way, and soon made themselves liked by their staff and their neighbours.

Monsieur died of apoplexy two years later, for as his new profession kept him in idleness and without any exercise, he had grown excessively stout, and his health had suffered. Since she had been a widow, all the frequenters of the establishment had wanted her; but people said that personally she was quite virtuous, and even the girls in the house could not discover anything against her. She was tall, stout and affable, and her complexion, which had become pale in the dimness of her house, the shutters of which were scarcely ever opened, shone as if it had been varnished. She had a fringe of curly, false hair, which gave her a juvenile look, that contrasted strongly with the ripeness of her figure. She was always smiling and cheerful, and was fond of a joke, but there was a shade of reserve about her, which her new occupation had not quite made her lose. Coarse words always shocked her, and when any young fellow who had been badly brought up called her establishment by its right name, she was angry and disgusted.

In a word, she had a refined mind, and although she treated her women as friends, yet she very frequently used to say that "she and they were not made of the same stuff."

Sometimes during the week, she would hire a carriage and take some of her girls into the country, where they used to enjoy themselves on the grass by the side of the little river. They were like a lot of girls let out from a school, and used to run races, and play childish games. They had a cold dinner on the grass, and drank cider, and went home at night with a delicious feeling of fatigue, and in the carriage they kissed Madame as their kind mother, who was full of goodness and complaisance.

The house had two entrances. At the corner there was a sort of low café, which sailors and the lower orders frequented at night, and she had two girls whose special duty it was to attend to that part of the business. With the assistance of the waiter, whose name was Frédéric, and who was a short, light-haired, beardless fellow, as strong as a horse, they set the half bottles of wine and the jugs of beer on the shaky marble tables, and then, sitting astride on the customers' knees, they urged them to drink.

The three other girls (there were only five of them) formed a kind of aristocracy, and were reserved for the company on the first floor, unless they were wanted downstairs, and there was nobody on the first floor. The Jupiter room, where the better classes used to meet, was papered in blue, and embellished with a large drawing representing Leda stretched out under the swan. That room was reached by a winding staircase, which ended at a narrow door opening on to the street, and above it, all night long a little lamp burned, behind wire bars, such as one still sees in some towns, at the foot of some shrine of a saint.

The house, which was old and damp, rather smelled of mildew. At times there was an odour of Eau de Cologne in the passages, or a half open door downstairs admitted the noise of the common men sitting and drinking downstairs, to the first floor, much to the disgust of the gentlemen who were there. Madame, who was familiar with those of her customers with whom she was on friendly terms, never left the drawing-room, and took much interest in what was going on in the town, and they regularly told her all the news. Her serious conversation was a change from the ceaseless chatter of the three women; it was a rest from the obscene jokes of those stout individuals who every evening indulged in the common-place debauchery of drinking a glass of liquor in company with prostitutes.

The names of the girls on the first floor were Fernande, Raphaële, and Rosa la Rosse. As the staff was limited, Madame had endeavoured that each member of it should be a pattern, an epitome of the feminine type, so that every customer might find as nearly as possible the realization of his ideal. Fernande represented the handsome blonde; she was very tall, rather fat, and lazy; a country girl, who could not get rid of her freckles, and whose short, light, almost colourless, tow-like hair, which was like combed-out flax, barely covered her head.

Raphaële, who came from Marseilles, a regular seaport street-walker, played the indispensable part of the handsome Jewess, and was thin, with high cheek bones, which were covered with rouge, and her black hair, which was always covered with pomade, fell in curls on her forehead. Her eyes would have been handsome, if the right one had not had a speck in it. Her Roman nose came down over a square jaw, where two false upper teeth contrasted strangely with the bad colour of the rest.

Rosa la Rosse was a little roll of fat, nearly all stomach, with very short legs, and from morning till night she sang songs, which were alternately indecent or sentimental, in a harsh voice, told silly, interminable tales, and only stopped talking in order to eat, and left off eating in order to talk; she was never still, and was active as a squirrel, in spite of her fat, and of her short legs; and her laugh, which was a torrent of shrill cries, resounded here and there, ceaselessly, in a bedroom, in the attic, in the café, everywhere, and about nothing.

The two women on the ground floor, Louise, who was nicknamed Cocote, and Flora, whom they called Balançoire, because she limped a little, looked like kitchen-maids dressed up for the carnival. The former always dressed as Liberty, with a tri-coloured sash, and the other as a Spanish woman, with a string of copper coins, which jingled at every step she took, in her carroty hair. They were like all other women of the lower orders, neither uglier nor better looking than they usually are. They looked just like servants at an inn, and they were generally called the two Pumps.

A jealous peace, which was, however, very rarely

disturbed, reigned among these five women, thanks to Madame's conciliatory wisdom, and to her constant good humour, and the establishment, which was the only one of the kind in the little town, was very much frequented. Madame had succeeded in giving it such a respectable appearance, she was so amiable and obliging to everybody, her good heart was so well known, that she was treated with a certain amount of consideration. The regular customers went out of their way to be nice to her, and were delighted when she was especially friendly towards them, and when they met during the day, they would say: "Until this evening, you know where," just as men say: "At the café, after dinner." In a word, Madame Tellier's house was somewhere to go to, and they very rarely missed their daily meetings there.

One evening, towards the end of May, the first arrival, Monsieur Poulin, who was a timber merchant, and had been mayor, found the door shut. The little lantern behind the grating was not alight; there was not a sound in the house; everything seemed dead. He knocked, gently at first, but then more loudly, but nobody answered the door. Then he went slowly up the street, and when he got to the market place, he met Monsieur Duvert, the shipbuilder, who was going to the same place, so they went back together, but did not meet with any better success. But suddenly they heard a loud noise close to them, and on going round the house, they saw a number of English and French sailors, who were hammering at the closed shutters of the café with their fists.

The two gentlemen immediately made their escape, for fear of being compromised, but a low "Pst" stopped them; it was Monsieur Tournevau, the fish curer, who had recognized them, and was trying to attract their attention. They told him what had happened, and he was all the more vexed at it, as he, a married man, and father of a family, only went there on Saturdays, *securitatis causa*, as he said, alluding to a measure of sanitary policy, which his friend Doctor Borde had advised him to observe. That was his regular evening, and now he should be deprived of it for the whole week.

The three men went as far as the quay together, and on the way they met young Monsieur Philippe, the banker's son, who frequented the place regularly, and Monsieur Pinipesse, the Collector of Taxes, and they all returned together by the street known as "the Ghetto," to make a last attempt. But the exasperated sailors were besieging the house, throwing stones at the shutters, and shouting, and the five first-floor customers went away as quickly as possible, and walked aimlessly about the streets.

Presently they met Monsieur Dupuis, the insurance agent, and then Monsieur Vasse, the Judge of the Tribunal of Commerce, and they took a long walk, going to the pier first of all, where they sat down in a row on the granite parapet, and watched the waves breaking. The foam on the crest of the waves gleamed a luminous white in the shadows, disappearing almost immediately, and the monotonous noise of the sea breaking on the rocks was prolonged through the darkness along the rocky shore.

When the sad promenaders had sat there for some time, Monsieur Tournevau said:

"This is not very amusing!"

"Decidedly not," Monsieur Pinipesse replied, and they started off again slowly.

After going through the street, which is called Sous-le-Bois, at the foot of the hill, they returned over the wooden bridge which crosses the Retenue, passed close to the railway, and came out again on to the market place, when suddenly a quarrel arose between Monsieur Pinipesse, the Collector of Taxes, and Monsieur Tournevau, about an edible fungus which one of them declared he had found in the neighbourhood.

As they were out of temper already from sheer boredom, they would very probably have come to blows, if the others had not interfered. Monsieur Pinipesse went off furious, and soon another altercation arose between the ex-mayor, Monsieur Poulin, and Monsieur Dupuis, the insurance agent, on the subject of the tax collector's salary, and the profits which he might make. Insulting remarks were freely passing between them, when a torrent of formidable cries was heard, and the body of sailors, who were tired of waiting so long outside a closed house, came into the square. They were walking arm-in-arm, two and two, and formed a long procession, and were shouting furiously. The landsmen went and hid themselves under a gateway, and the yelling crew disappeared in the direction of the abbey. For a long time they still heard the noise, which diminished like a storm in the distance, and then silence was restored, and Monsieur Poulin and Monsieur Dupuis, who were enraged with each other, went in different directions, without wishing each other good-bye.

The other four set off again, and instinctively went in the direction of Madame Tellier's establishment, which was still closed, silent, impenetrable. A quiet, but obstinate, drunken man was knocking at the door of the café, and then stopped and called Frédéric, the waiter, in a low voice, but finding that he got no answer, he sat down on the doorstep, and waited the course of events.

The others were just going to retire, when the noisy band of sailors reappeared at the end of the street. The French sailors were shouting the *Marseillaise*, and the Englishmen, *Rule Britannia*. There was a general lurching against the wall, and then the drunken brutes went on their way towards the quay, where a fight broke out between the two nations, in the course of which an Englishman had his arm broken, and a Frenchman his nose split.

The drunken man, who had stopped outside the door, was crying by that time, as drunken men and children cry, when they are vexed, and the others went away. By degrees, calm was restored in the noisy town; here and there, at moments, the distant sound of voices could be heard, and then died away in the distance.

One man, only, was still wandering about, Monsieur Tournevau, the fish curer, who was vexed at having to wait until the next Saturday, and he hoped for something to turn up, he did not know what; but he was exasperated at the police for thus allowing an establishment of such public utility, which they had under their control, to be closed.

He went back to it, examining the walls, and trying to find out the reason, and on the shutter he saw a notice stuck up, so he struck a wax vesta, and read the following in a large, uneven hand: "Closed on account of Confirmation."

Then he went away, as he saw it was useless to remain, and left the drunken man lying on the pavement fast asleep, outside that inhospitable door.

The next day, all the regular customers, one after the other, found some reason for going through the street with a bundle of papers under their arm, to keep them in countenance, and with a furtive glance they all read that mysterious notice:

Closed on account of Confirmation.

PART II

The fact is, Madame had a brother, who was a carpenter in their native place, Virville in the Department of Eure. When Madame had still kept the inn at Yvetot, she had stood godmother to that brother's daughter, who had received the name of Constance, Constance Rivet; she herself being a Rivet on her father's side. The carpenter, who knew that his sister was in a good position, did not lose sight of her, although they did not meet often, for they were both kept at home by their occupations, and lived a long way from each other. But as the girl was twelve years old, and going to be confirmed, he seized that opportunity of coming together, and wrote to his sister that he was counting on her for the ceremony. Their old parents were dead, and as she could not well refuse, she accepted the invitation. Her brother, whose name was Joseph, hoped that by dint of showing his sister attentions, she might be induced to make her will in the girl's favour, as she had no children of her own.

His sister's occupation did not trouble his scruples in the least, and besides, nobody knew anything about it in Virville. When they spoke of her, they only said: "Madame Tellier is living at Fécamp," which might mean that she was living on her own private income. It was quite twenty miles from Fécamp to Virville, and for a peasant, twenty miles on land are more than is crossing the ocean to an educated person. The people at Virville had never been farther than Rouen, and nothing attracted the people from Fécamp to a village of five hundred houses, in the middle of a plain, and situated in another department, and, at any rate, nothing was known about her business.

But the Confirmation was coming on, and Madame was in great embarrassment. She had no under mistress, and did not care to leave her house, even for a day, for all the rivalries between the girls upstairs and those downstairs, would infallibly break out; no doubt Frédéric would get drunk, and when he was in that state he would knock anybody down for a mere word. At last, however, she made up her mind to take them all with her, with the exception of the man, to whom she gave a holiday, until the next day but one.

When she asked her brother, he made no objection, but undertook to put them all up for a night, and so on Saturday morning, the eight o'clock express carried off Madame and her companions in a second-class carriage. As far as Beuzeille, they were alone, and chattered like magpies, but at that station a couple got in. The man, an old peasant, dressed in a blue blouse with a folding collar, wide sleeves, tight at the wrist, and ornamented with white embroidery, wore an old high hat whose long rusty nap seemed to stand on end, held an enormous green umbrella in one hand, and a large basket in the other, from which the heads of three frightened ducks protruded. The woman, who sat stiffly in her rustic finery, had a face like a fowl, and with a nose that was as pointed as a bill. She sat down opposite her husband and did not stir, as she was startled at finding herself in such smart company.

There was certainly an array of striking colours in the carriage. Madame was dressed in blue silk from head to foot, and had on over her dress a dazzling red shawl of imitation French cashmere. Fernande was panting in a Scottish plaid dress, whose bodice, which her companions had laced as tight as they could, had forced up her falling bosom into a double dome, that was continually heaving up and down, and which seemed liquid beneath the material. Raphaële, with a bonnet covered with feathers, so that it looked like a nest full of birds, had on a lilac dress with gold spots on it, and there was something Oriental about it that suited her Jewish face. Rosa la Rosse had on a pink petticoat with large flounces, and looked like a very fat child, an obese dwarf; while the two Pumps looked as if they had cut their dresses out of old, flowered curtains, dating from the Restoration.

As soon as they were no longer alone in the compartment, the ladies put on staid looks, and began to talk of subjects which might give the others a high opinion of them. But at Bolbec a gentleman with light whiskers, wearing a gold chain, and two or three rings, got in, and put several parcels wrapped in oilcloth into the net over his head. He looked inclined for a joke, and a good-natured fellow. He saluted, smiled, and said affably:

"Are you ladies changing to another garrison?"

This question embarrassed them all considerably. Madame, however, quickly recovered her composure, and said sharply, to avenge the honour of her corps:

"I think you might try and be polite!"

He excused himself, and said: "I beg your pardon, I ought to have said nunnery."

As Madame could not think of a retort, or perhaps as she thought herself justified sufficiently, she gave him a dignified bow, and pinched in her lips.

Then the gentleman, who was sitting between Rosa la Rosse and the old peasant, began to wink knowingly at the ducks, whose heads were sticking out of the basket, and when he felt that he had fixed the attention of his public, he began to tickle them under their bills, and spoke funnily to them, to make the company smile.

"We have left our little pond, quack! quack! to make the acquaintance of the little spit, qu-ack! qu-ack!"

The unfortunate creatures turned their necks away, to avoid his caresses, and made desperate efforts to get out of their wicker prison, and then, suddenly, all at once, uttered the most lamentable quacks of distress. The women exploded with laughter. They leaned forward and pushed each other, so as to see better; they were very much interested in the ducks, and the gentleman redoubled his airs, his wit, and his teasing.

Rosa joined in, and leaning over her neighbour's legs, she kissed the three animals on the head, and immediately all the girls wanted to kiss them in turn, and the gentleman took them on to his knees, made them jump up and down and pinched them. The two peasants, who were even in greater consternation than their poultry, rolled their eyes as if they were possessed, without venturing to move, and their old wrinkled faces had not a smile nor a movement.

Then the gentleman, who was a commercial traveller, offered the ladies braces by way of a joke, and taking up one of his packages, he opened it. It was a trick, for the parcel contained garters. There were blue silk, pink silk, red silk, violet silk, mauve silk garters, and the buckles were made of two gilt metal Cupids, embracing each other. The girls uttered exclamations of delight and looked at them with that gravity which is natural to a woman when she is hankering after a bargain. They consulted one another by their looks or in a whisper, and replied in the same manner, and Madame was longingly handling a pair of orange garters that were broader and more imposing looking than the rest; really fit for the mistress of such an establishment.

The gentleman waited, for a bright idea had struck him.

"Come, my dears," he said, "you must try them on."

There was a storm of exclamations, and they squeezed their petticoats between their legs, as if they thought he was going to ravish them, but he quietly waited his time, and said: "Well, if you will not, I shall pack them up again."

And he added cunningly: "I offer any pair they like, to those who will try them on."

But they would not, and sat up very straight, and looked dignified.

But the two Pumps looked so distressed that he renewed the offer to them, and Flora Balançoire especially visibly hesitated. He pressed her: "Come, my dear, a little courage! Just look at that lilac pair; it will suit your dress admirably . . ."

That decided her, and pulling up her dress she showed a thick leg fit for a milkmaid, in a badly-fitting, coarse stocking. The commercial traveller stooped down and fastened the garter below the knee first of all and then above it; and he tickled the girl gently, which made her scream and jump. When he had done, he gave her the lilac pair, and asked: "Who next?"

"I! I!" they all shouted at once, and he began

on Rosa la Rosse, who uncovered a shapeless, round thing without any ankle, a regular "sausage of a leg," as Raphaële used to say.

The commercial traveller complimented Fernande, and grew quite enthusiastic over her powerful columns.

The thin tibias of the handsome Jewess met with less success, and Louise Cocote, by way of a joke, put her petticoats over his head, so that Madame was obliged to interfere to check such unseemly behaviour.

Lastly, Madame herself put out her leg, a handsome, Norman leg, muscular and plump, and in his surprise and pleasure, the commercial traveller gallantly took off his hat to salute that master calf, like a true French cavalier.

The two peasants, who were speechless from surprise, looked aside, out of the corners of their eyes, and they looked so exactly like fowls that the man with the light whiskers, when he sat up, said "cock-a-doodle-do!" under their very noses, and that gave rise to another storm of amusement.

The old people got out at Motteville, with their basket, their ducks, and their umbrella, and they heard the woman say to her husband, as they went away:

"They are bad women, who are off to that cursed place Paris."

The funny commercial traveller himself got out at Rouen, after behaving so coarsely, that Madame was obliged sharply to put him into his right place, and she added, as a moral: "This will teach us not to talk to the first-comer."

At Oissel they changed trains, and at a little station farther on, Monsieur Joseph Rivet was waiting for them with a large cart and a number of chairs in it, which was drawn by a white horse.

The carpenter politely kissed all the ladies, and then helped them into his conveyance.

Three of them sat on three chairs at the back, Raphaële, Madame and her brother on the three chairs in front, and Rosa, who had no seat, settled herself as comfortably as she could on tall Fernande's knees, and then they set off.

But the horse's jerky trot shook the cart so terribly that the chairs began to dance, throwing the travellers into the air, to the right and to the left, as if they had been dancing puppets, which made them make frightened grimaces, and scream with fear. But this was suddenly cut short by another jolt of the cart.

They clung on to the sides of the vehicle, their bonnets fell on to their backs, their noses on their shoulders, and the white horse went on stretching out his head, and holding out his tail quite straight, a little, hairless rat's tail, with which he whisked his buttocks from time to time.

Joseph Rivet, with one leg on the shafts and the other bent under him, held out the reins with his elbows very high, and he kept uttering a kind of chuckling sound, which made the horse prick up its ears and go faster.

The green country extended on either side of the road, and here and there the colza in flower presented a waving expanse of yellow, from which there arose a strong, wholesome, sweet and penetrating smell, which the wind carried to some distance. Cornflowers showed their little blue heads among the tall rye, and the women wanted to pick them, but Monsieur Rivet refused to stop. Then sometimes a whole field appeared to be covered with blood, so thickly were the poppies growing, and the cart, which looked as if it were filled with flowers of more brilliant hue, drove on through the fields coloured with wild flowers, and disappeared behind the trees of a farm, only to reappear and to go on again through the yellow or green standing crops, studded with red or blue, a dazzling carload of women, fleeing beneath the sun.

One o'clock struck as they drove up to the carpenter's door. They were tired out, and pale with hunger, as they had eaten nothing since they left home, and Madame Rivet ran out, and made them alight, one after another, and kissed them as soon as they were on the ground, and she seemed as if she would never tire of kissing her sister-in-law, whom she apparently wanted to monopolize. They had lunch in the workshop, which had been cleared out for the next day's dinner.

A capital omelette, followed by fried eel, and washed down by good, sharp cider, made them all feel comfortable.

Rivet had taken a glass so that he might drink their health, and his wife cooked, waited on them, brought in the dishes, took them out, and asked all of them in a whisper whether they had everything they wanted. A number of boards standing against the walls, and heaps of shavings that had been swept into the corners, gave out a smell of planed wood, or carpentering, that resinous odour which penetrates the lungs.

They wanted to see the little girl, but she had gone to church, and would not be back until evening, so they all went out for a stroll in the country.

It was a small village, through which the high road passed. Ten or a dozen houses on either side of the single street, were inhabited by the butcher, the grocer, the carpenter, the innkeeper, the shoemaker, and the baker.

The church was at the end of the street, and was surrounded by a small churchyard, and four enormous lime-trees, which stood just outside the porch, shaded it completely. It was built of flint, in no particular style, and had a slated steeple. Beyond it, the open country began again, broken here and there by clumps of trees which hid the homestead.

Although he was in his working clothes, Rivet had given his arm to his sister, out of politeness, and was walking with her majestically. His wife, who was overwhelmed by Raphaële's gold-spangled dress, was walking between her and Fernande, and fat Rosa was trotting behind with Louise Cocote and Flora Balançoire, who was limping along, quite tired out.

The inhabitants came to their doors, the children left off playing, and a window curtain would be raised, revealing a muslin cap, while an old woman with a crutch, and who was almost blind, crossed herself as if it were a religious procession, and they all looked for a long time after those handsome ladies from the town, who had come so far to be present at the confirmation of Joseph Rivet's little girl, and the carpenter rose very much in the public estimation.

As they passed the church, they heard some children singing; little shrill voices were singing a hymn, but Madame would not let them go in, for fear of disturbing the little cherubs.

After a walk, during which Joseph Rivet enumerated the principal landed proprietors, spoke about the yield of the land, and productiveness of the cows and sheep, he took his herd of women home and installed them in his house, and as it was very small, they had put them into the rooms, two by two.

Just for once, Rivet would sleep in the workshop on the shavings; his wife was going to share her bed with her sister-in-law, and Fernande and Raphaële were to sleep together in the next room. Louise and Flora were put into the kitchen, where they had a mattress on the floor, and Rosa had a little dark cupboard at the top of the stairs to herself, close to the loft, where the candidate for confirmation was to sleep.

When the girl came in, she was overwhelmed with kisses; all the women wished to caress her, with that need of tender expansion, that professional habit of wheedling, which had made them kiss the ducks in the railway carriage.

They all took her on to their laps, stroked her soft, light hair, and pressed her in their arms with vehement and spontaneous outbursts of affection, and the child, who was very good and religious, bore it all patiently.

As the day had been a fatiguing one for everybody, they all went to bed soon after dinner. The whole village was wrapped in that perfect stillness of the country, which is almost like a religious silence, and the girls, who were accustomed to the noisy evenings of their establishment, felt rather impressed by the perfect repose of the sleeping village, and they shivered, not with cold, but with those little shivers of solitude which come over uneasy and troubled hearts.

As soon as they were in bed, two and two together, they clasped each other in their arms, as if to protect themselves against this feeling of the calm and profound slumber of the earth. But Rosa la Rosse, who was alone in her little dark cupboard, and was not accustomed to sleep alone, felt a vague and painful emotion come over her.

She was tossing about in bed, unable to get to sleep, when she heard the faint sobs of a crying child close to her head through the partition. She was frightened, and called out, and was answered by a weak voice, broken by sobs. It was the little girl, who was always used to sleeping in her mother's room, and who was frightened in her small attic.

Rosa was delighted, got up softly so as not to awaken anyone, and went and fetched the child. She took her into her warm bed, kissed her and pressed her to her bosom, cossetted her, lavished exaggerated manifestations of tenderness on her, and at last grew calmer herself and went to sleep. And till morning, the candidate for confirmation slept with her head on the prostitute's naked bosom.

At five o'clock, the little church bell ringing the *Angelus*, woke the women up, who usually slept the whole morning long, their only rest after the fatigues of the night. The peasants were up already, and the women went busily from house to house, talking animatedly, carefully bringing short, starched, muslin dresses in bandboxes, or very long wax tapers, with a bow of silk fringed with gold in the middle, and with dents in the wax for the fingers.

The sun was already high in the blue sky, which still had a rosy tint towards the horizon, like a faint trace of dawn remaining. Families of fowls were walking about outside the houses, and here and there a black cock, with a glistening breast, raised his head, which was crowned by his red comb, flapped his wings, and uttered his shrill crow, which the other cocks repeated.

Vehicles of all sorts came from neighbouring parishes, and discharged tall, Norman women, in dark dresses, with neckerchiefs crossed over the bosom, which were fastened with silver brooches, a hundred years old. The men had put on their blouses over their new frock-coats, or over their old dress-coats of green cloth, the two tails of which hung down below their blouses. When the horses were in the stable, there was a double line of rustic conveyances along the road; carts, cabriolets, tilburies, char-à-bancs, traps of every shape and age, resting on their shafts, or else with them in the air.

The carpenter's house was as busy as a beehive. The ladies, in dressing-jackets and petticoats, with their hanging down, thin, short hair, which looked as if it were faded and worn by use, were busy dressing the child, who was standing motionless on a table, while Madame Tellier was directing the movements of her flying column. They washed her, did her hair, dressed her, and with the help of a number of pins, they arranged the folds of her dress, and took in the waist, which was too large, and made her look as elegant as possible. Then, when she was ready, she was told to sit down and not to move, and the crowd of excited women hurried off to get ready themselves.

The bell of the little church began to ring again, and its poor tinkle was lost in the air, like a feeble voice which is soon drowned in space. The candidates came out of the houses, and went towards the parochial building which contained the two schools and the town hall and stood quiet at one end of the village, while the "House of God" was situated at the other.

The parents, in their very best clothes, followed their children, with awkward looks, and those clumsy movements of bodies always bent at work. The little girls disappeared in a cloud of muslin, which looked like whipped cream, while the lads, who looked like embryo waiters, and whose heads shone with pomade, walked with their legs apart, so as not to get any dust or dirt on their black trousers.

It was something for the family to be proud of, when a large number of relations, who had come from a distance, surrounded the child, and, consequently, the carpenter's triumph was complete. Madame Tellier's regiment, with its mistress at its head, followed Constance; her father gave his arm to his sister, her mother walked by the side of Raphaële, Fernande, with Rosa and the two Pumps together, and thus they walked majestically through the village, like a general's staff in full uniform, while the effect on the village was startling.

At the school, the girls arranged themselves under the Sister of Mercy, and the boys under the schoolmaster, a handsome man, who looked well, and they started off, singing a hymn as they went. The boys led the way, in two files, between the two rows of unyoked vehicles, and the girls followed in the same order; and as all the people in the village had given the town ladies the precedence out of politeness, they came immediately behind the girls, and lengthened the double line of the procession still more, three on the right and three on the left, while their dresses were as striking as the set piece in a firework display.

When they went into the church, the congregation grew quite excited. They pressed against each other, they turned round, they jostled one another in order to see, and some of the devout ones spoke almost aloud, as they were so astonished at the sight of those ladies whose dresses were more trimmed than the chasubles of the choir-boys.

The Mayor offered them his pew, the first one on the right, close to the choir, and Madame Tellier sat there with her sister-in-law, Fernande and Raphaële, Rosa la Rosse, and the two Pumps occupied the second seat, in company with the carpenter.

The choir was full of kneeling children, the girls on one side, and the boys on the other, and the long wax tapers which they held looked like lances, pointing in all directions, and three men were standing in front of the lectern, singing as loud as they could. They prolonged the syllables of the sonorous Latin indefinitely, holding on to *Amens* with interminable *a — a's*, while the serpent kept up the monotonous, long drawn out notes, which that long-throated, copper instrument uttered. A child's shrill voice took up the reply, and from time to time a priest sitting in a stall and wearing a square biretta, got up, muttered something, and sat down again, while the three singers continued, with their eyes fixed on the big book of plain-song lying open before them on the outstretched wings of an eagle, mounted on a pivot.

Then silence ensued. The whole congregation knelt with one movement, and the celebrant appeared, old and venerable, with white hair, bent over the chalice which he carried in his left hand. Two assistants in red robes walked in front of him, and behind appeared a crowd of choristers in heavy clogs, who lined up on both sides of the choir.

A small bell chimed amidst dead silence. The service began. The priest moved slowly back and forth in front of the tabernacle of gold, genuflecting, intoning in a cracked voice, lisping with age, the preliminary prayers. As soon as he stopped all the choristers and the organ burst forth simultaneously, and in the congregation men also sang, not so loudly, more humbly, as befits mere spectators. Suddenly the *Kyrie eleison* rose to the heavens from every heart and throat. Grains of dust and fragments of mouldering wood actually fell from the ancient arch which was shaken by this explosion of sound. The sun beating on the slates of the roof turned the little church into a furnace. A great emotion, an anxious wait, the imminence of the ineffable mystery, filled the hearts of the children with awe, and touched the breasts of their mothers.

The priest, who had remained seated for some time, walked up again towards the altar and, bareheaded, with his silvery hair, he approached the supernatural act with trembling gestures. He turned towards the faithful and, spreading out his hands, pronounced the words: "*Orate, fratres,*" "pray, brethren." They all prayed. The old priest was now uttering in a stammering whisper the mysterious and supreme words; the bell chimed several times in succession; the prostrate crowd called upon God; the children were fainting from boundless anxiety.

It was then that Rosa, with her head in both her hands, suddenly thought of her mother and her village church on her first communion. She almost fancied that that day had returned, when she was so small, and almost hidden in her white dress, and she began to cry.

First of all, she wept silently, and the tears dropped slowly from her eyes, but her emotion increased with her recollections, and she began to sob. She took out her pocket-handkerchief, wiped her eyes, and held it to her mouth, so as not to scream, but it was useless. A sort of rattle escaped her throat, and she was answered by two other profound, heart-breaking sobs; for her two neighbours, Louise and Flora, who were kneeling near her, overcome by similar recollections, were sobbing by her side, amidst a flood of tears, and as tears are contagious, Madame soon in turn found that her eyes were wet, and on turning to her sister-in-law, she saw that all the occupants of her seat were also crying.

The priest was creating the body of Christ. The children were unconscious of everything, prostrated on the tiled floor by burning devotion, and throughout the church, here and there, a wife, a mother, a sister, seized by the strange sympathy of poignant emotion, and agitated by those handsome ladies on their knees, who were shaken by their sobs, was moistening her checked cotton handkerchief, and pressing her beating heart with her left hand.

Just as the sparks from an engine will set fire to dry grass, so the tears of Rosa and of her companions infected the whole congregation in a moment. Men, women, old men, and lads in new blouses were soon all sobbing, and something superhuman seemed to be hovering over their heads; a spirit, the powerful breath of an invisible and all-powerful being.

Then, in the choir a sharp short noise resounded. The Sister of Mercy had given the signal for communion by striking on her prayer-book, and the children, shivering with a divine fever, approached the holy table. A whole row knelt down. The old priest, holding in his hand the pyx of gilt silver, walked in front of them, administering the sacred host, the body of Christ, the salvation of the world. They opened their mouths convulsively, with nervous grimaces, their eyes shut and their faces deathly pale. And the long communion altar cloth, spread out beneath their chins, quivered like running water.

Suddenly a species of madness seemed to pervade the church, the noise of a crowd in a state of frenzy, a tempest of sobs and stifled cries. It passed through them like gusts of wind which bow the trees in a forest, and the priest remained standing, motionless, the host in his hand, paralysed by emotion, saying: "It is God, it is God who is amongst us, manifesting his presence. He is descending upon his kneeling people in reply to my prayers." He stammered out incoherent prayers, without finding words, prayers of the soul, when it soars towards heaven.

He finished giving communion in such a state of religious exaltation that his legs shook under him, and when he himself had partaken of the blood of the Lord, he plunged into a prayer of ecstatic thanks.

The people behind him gradually grew calmer. The choristers, in all the dignity of their white surplices, went on in somewhat uncertain voices, and the serpent itself seemed hoarse, as if the instrument had been weeping.

Raising his hands the priest then made a sign to them to be silent, and passing between the two lines of communicants plunged in an ecstasy of happiness, he went up to the chancel steps. The congregation sat down amidst the noise of chairs, and they all blew their noses violently. As soon as they saw the priest, there was silence, and he began to speak in low, muffled, hesitating tones: "My dear brethren and sisters, and children, I thank you from the bottom of my heart. You have just given me the greatest joy of my life. I felt that God was coming down amongst us in response to my call. He came, he was there, present, filling your souls, causing your tears to overflow. I am the oldest priest in the diocese, and to-day I am the happiest. A miracle has taken place among us, a true, a great, a sublime miracle. While Jesus Christ was entering the bodies of these little children for the first time, the Holy Spirit, the celestial bird, the breath of God descended upon you, possessed you, seized you, and bent you like reeds in the wind."

Then, in firmer tones, turning towards the two pews where the carpenter's guests were seated:

"I especially thank you, my dear sisters, who have come from such a distance, and whose presence among us, whose evident faith and ardent piety have set such a salutary example to all. You have edified my parish; your emotion has warmed all hearts; without you, this great day would not, perhaps, have had this really divine character. It is sufficient, at times, that there should be one chosen to keep in the flock, to make the whole flock blessed."

His voice failed him from emotion. He added: "I pray for grace for you. Amen." And he returned to the altar to conclude the service.

Then they all left the church as quickly as possible, and the children themselves were restless, as they were tired with such a prolonged tension of the mind. Besides that, they were hungry, and by degrees the parents left without waiting for the last gospel, to see about dinner.

There was a crowd outside, a noisy crowd, a babel of loud voices, where the shrill Norman accent was discernible. The villagers formed two ranks, and when the children appeared, each family seized its own.

The whole houseful of women caught hold of Constance, surrounded her and kissed her, and Rosa was especially demonstrative. At last she took hold of one hand, while Madame Tellier held the other, and Raphaële and Fernande held up her long muslin petticoat, so that it might not drag in the dust; Louise and Flora brought up the rear with Madame Rivet, and the child, who was very silent and thoughtful, filled with the sense of God whom she had absorbed, set off home, in the midst of this guard of honour.

The dinner was served in the workshop, on long boards supported by trestles, and through the open door they could see all the enjoyment that was going on. Everywhere they were feasting, and through every window were to be seen tables surrounded by people in their Sunday best, and a cheerful noise was heard in every house, while the men were sitting in their shirt-sleeves, drinking pure cider, glass after glass, and in the middle of each company two children could be seen, here two boys, there two girls, dining one with the family of the other.

In the carpenter's house, their gaiety maintained somewhat of an air of reserve, which was the consequence of the emotion of the girls in the morning, and Rivet was the only one who was in a good form, and he was drinking to excess. Madame Tellier was looking at the clock every moment, for, in order not to lose two days following, they ought to take the 3:55 train, which would bring them to Fécamp towards evening.

The carpenter tried very hard to distract her attention, so as to keep his guests until the next day, but he did not succeed, for she never joked when there was business to be done, and as soon as they had had their coffee she ordered her girls to make haste and get ready, and then, turning to her brother, she said:

"You must have the horses put in immediately," and she herself went to finish her last preparations.

When she came down again, her sister-in-law was waiting to speak to her about the child, and a long conversation took place, in which, however, nothing was settled. The carpenter's wife finished, and pretended to be very much moved, and Madame Tellier, who was holding the girl on her knees, would not pledge herself to anything definite, but merely gave vague promises . . . she would not forget her, there was plenty of time, and then, they would meet again.

But the conveyance did not come to the door, and the women did not come downstairs. Upstairs, they even heard loud laughter, falls, little screams, and much clapping of hands, and so, while the carpenter's wife went to the stable to see whether the cart was ready, Madame went upstairs.

Rivet, who was very drunk, and half undressed, was vainly trying to violate Rosa, who was dying with laughter. The two Pumps were holding him by the arms and trying to calm him, as they were shocked at such a scene after that morning's ceremony; but Raphaële and Fernande were urging him on, writhing and holding their sides with laughter, and they uttered shrill cries at every useless attempt that the drunken fellow made. The man was furious, his face was red, he was all unbuttoned, and he was trying to shake off the two women who were clinging to him, while he was pulling at Rosa's dress with all his might and muttering: "So you won't, you hussy?"

But Madame, who was very indignant, went up to her brother, seized him by the shoulders, and threw him out of the room with such violence that he fell against a wall in the passage, and a minute afterwards they heard him pumping water on to his head in the yard, and when he came back with the cart, he was quite calm.

They returned the same way as they had come the day before, and the little white horse started off, with his quick, dancing trot. Under the hot sun, their fun, which had been checked during dinner, broke out again. The girls were now amused at the jolts which the wagon gave, pushed their neighbour's chairs, and burst out laughing every moment, for they were in the vein for it, after Rivet's vain attempt.

There was a haze over the country, the roads were glaring, and dazzled their eyes, and the wheels raised up two trails of dust, which followed the cart for a long time along the high road, and presently Fernande, who was fond of music, asked Rosa to sing something, and she boldly struck up the *Gros Curé de Meudon*, but Madame made her stop immediately, as she thought it a song which was very unsuitable for such a day, and she added:

"Sing us something of Béranger's." And so, after a moment's hesitation, she began Béranger's song, *The Grandmother*, in her worn-out voice:

Ma grand'mère, un soir à sa fête,
De vin pur ayant bu deux doigts,
Nous disait, en branlant la tête:
Que d'amoureux j'eus autrefois!

Combien je regrette
Mon bras si dodu,
Ma jambe bien faite,
Et le temps perdu!

And the girls in chorus, led by Madame, repeated the refrain:

Combien je regrette
Mon bras si dodu,
Ma jambe bien faite,
Et le temps perdu!

"That's fine!" declared Rivet, carried away by the rhythm, and Rosa went on at once:

Quoi, maman, vous n'étiez pas sage?
— Non, vraiment! et de mes appas,
Seule, à quinze ans, j'appris l'usage,
Car la nuit, je ne dormais pas.

They all shouted the refrain to every verse, while Rivet beat time on the shafts with his foot, and on the horse's back with the reins, who, as if he himself were carried away by the rhythm, broke into a wild gallop, and threw all the women in a heap, one on the top of the other, on the bottom of the conveyance.

They got up, laughing wildly, and the song went on, shouted at the top of their voices, beneath the burning sky, among the ripening grain, to the rapid gallop of the little horse, who set off every time the refrain was sung, and galloped a hundred yards, to their great delight, while occasionally a stone breaker by the roadside sat up and looked at the wild and shouting female load through his wire spectacles.

When they got out at the station, the carpenter said:

"I am sorry you are going; we might have had some fun together." But Madame replied very sensibly: "Everything has its right time, and we cannot always be enjoying ourselves." And then he had a sudden inspiration:

"Look here, I will come and see you at Fécamp next month." And he gave a knowing look, with a bright and roguish eye.

"Come," Madame said, "you must be sensible; you may come if you like, but you are not to be up to any of your tricks."

He did not reply, and as they heard the whistle of the train, he immediately began to kiss them all. When he came to Rosa's turn, he tried to get to her mouth, which she, however, smiling with her lips closed, turned away from him each time by a rapid movement of her head to one side. He held her in his arms, but he could not attain his object, as his large whip, which he was holding in his hand and waving behind the girl's back in desperation, interfered with his efforts.

"Passengers for Rouen, take your seats, please!" a guard cried, and they got in. There was a slight whistle, followed by a loud whistle, from the engine, which noisily puffed out its first jet of steam, while the wheels began to turn a little, with a visible effort, and Rivet left the station and went to the gate by the side of the line to get another look at Rosa, and as the carriage full of human merchandise passed him, he began to crack his whip and to jump, while he sang at the top of his voice:

Combien je regrette
Mon bras si dodu,
Ma jambe bien faite,
Et le temps perdu!

And then he watched a white pocket-handkerchief, which somebody was waving, as it disappeared in the distance.

PART III

THEY slept the peaceful sleep of a quiet conscience, until they got to Rouen, and when they returned to the house, refreshed and rested, Madame could not help saying:

"It was all very well, but I was already longing to get home."

They hurried over their supper, and then, when they had put on their professional costume, waited for their usual customers, and the little coloured lamp outside the door told the passers-by that the flock had returned to the fold, and in a moment the news spread, nobody knew how or by whom. Monsieur Phillippe, the banker's son, even carried his forgetfulness so far, as to send a special messenger to Monsieur Tournevau, who was confined to the bosom of his family.

The fish-curer used every Sunday to have several cousins to dinner, and they were having coffee, when a man came in with a letter in his hand. Monsieur Tournevau was much excited, he opened the envelope and grew pale; it only contained these words in pencil:

"*The cargo of cod has been found; the ship has come into port; good business for you. Come immediately.*"

He felt in his pockets, gave the messenger twopence, and suddenly blushing to his ears, he said: "I must go out." He handed his wife the laconic and mysterious note, rang the bell, and when the servant came in, he asked her to bring him his hat and overcoat immediately. As soon as he was in the street, he began to run, and the way seemed to him to be twice as long as usual, his impatience was so great.

Madame Tellier's establishment had put on quite a holiday look. On the ground floor, a number of sailors were making a deafening noise, and Louise and Flora drank with one and the other, so as to merit their name of the two Pumps more than ever. They were being called for everywhere at once; already they were not able to cope with business, and the night bid fair to be a very busy one for them.

The circle in the upstairs room was complete by nine o'clock. Monsieur Vasse, the Judge of the Tribunal of Commerce, Madame's usual, but Platonic wooer, was talking to her in a corner, in a low voice, and they were both smiling, as if they were about to come to an understanding. Monsieur Poulin, the ex-mayor, was holding Rosa astride on his knees; and she, with her nose close to his, was running her podgy hands through the old gentleman's white whiskers. A glimpse of her bare thigh was visible beneath her upraised dress of yellow silk, and was thrown into relief by the background of his dark trousers, while her red stockings were held up by blue garters, the commercial traveller's present.

Tall Fernande, who was lying on the sofa, had both her feet on Monsieur Pinipesse, the tax-collector's stomach, and her back on young Monsieur Philippe's waistcoat; her right arm was round his neck, while she held a cigarette in her left.

Raphaële appeared to be discussing matters with Monsieur Dupuis, the insurance agent, and she finished by saying: "Yes, my dear, I will, this evening." Then waltzing across the room,—"Anything you like this evening," she cried.

Just then, the door opened suddenly, and Monsieur Tournevau came in, who was greeted with enthusiastic cries of: "Long live Tournevau!" And Raphaële, who was still twirling round, went and threw herself into his arms. He seized her in a vigorous embrace, and without saying a word, lifting her up as if she had been a feather, he went through the room, opened the door at the other end and disappeared with his living burden in the direction of the stairs, amidst great applause.

Rosa, who was exciting the ex-mayor, kissing him every moment, and pulling both his whiskers at the same time in order to keep his head straight, was inspired by this example. "Come, do what he did," she said. The old boy got up, pulled his waistcoat straight, and followed the girl, fumbling in the pocket where he kept his money.

Fernande and Madame remained with the four men, and Monsieur Philippe exclaimed: "I will pay for some champagne; get three bottles, Madame Tellier." And Fernande gave him a hug, and whispered to him: "Play us a waltz, will you?" So he rose and sat down at the old piano in the corner, and managed to get a hoarse waltz out of the entrails of the instrument. The tall girl put her arms round the Tax-Collector, Madame fell into the arms of Monsieur Vasse, and the two couples turned round, kissing as they danced. Monsieur Vasse, who had formerly danced in good society, waltzed with such elegance that Madame was quite captivated. She looked at him with a glance which said "Yes," a more discreet and delicious "Yes" than the spoken word.

Frédéric brought the champagne; the first cork popped, and Monsieur Philippe played the introduction to a quadrille, through which the four dancers walked in society fashion, decorously, with propriety, deportment, bows and curtsies, and then they began to drink. Monsieur Tournevau returned, relieved, contented, radiant. "I do not know," he said, "what has happened to Raphaële; she is perfect this evening." A glass was handed to him and he drank it off at a gulp, as he murmured, "By heavens, everything is being done on a luxurious scale!"

Monsieur Philippe at once struck up a lively polka, and Monsieur Tournevau started off with the handsome Jewess, whom he held up in the air, without letting her feet touch the ground. Monsieur Pinipesse and Monsieur Vasse had started off with renewed vigour, and from time to time one or other couple would stop to toss off a long glass of sparkling wine, and the dance was threatening to become never-ending, when Rosa opened the door.

She had a candlestick in her hand, her hair was down, and she was in bedroom slippers and chemise. Her face was flushed and very animated: "I want to dance," she shouted. "And what about the old gentleman?" Raphaële asked. Rosa burst out laughing: "Him? he's asleep already. He falls asleep at once." She caught hold of Monsieur Dupuis, who was sitting on the sofa doing nothing, and the polka was resumed.

But the bottles were empty. "I will pay for one," Monsieur Tournevau said. "So will I," Monsieur Vasse declared. "And I will do the same," Monsieur Dupuis remarked.

They all began to clap their hands, and it soon became a regular ball, and from time to time, Louise and Flora ran upstairs quickly, had a few turns, while their customers downstairs grew impatient, and then they returned regretfully to the café. At midnight they were still dancing. From time to time one of the girls would disappear, and when she was wanted for the dance, it would suddenly be discovered that one of the men was also missing.

"Where have you been?" asked Monsieur Philippe, jocularly, when Monsieur Pinipesse returned with Fernande. "Watching Monsieur Poulin sleep," replied the Tax-Collector. The joke was a great success, and all the men in turn went upstairs to see Monsieur Poulin sleeping, with one or other of the girls, who on this occasion displayed an unusual amiability.

Madame shut her eyes to what was going on and she had long private talks in corners with Monsieur Vasse, as if to settle the last details of something that had already been settled.

At last, at one o'clock, the two married men, Monsieur Tournevau and Monsieur Pinipesse, declared that they were going home, and wanted to pay. Nothing was charged for except the champagne, and that only cost six francs a bottle, instead of ten, which was the usual price, and when they expressed their surprise at such generosity, Madame, who was beaming, said to them:

"We don't have a holiday every day."

STORY OF A FARM GIRL

AS the weather was very fine, the people on the farm had dined more speedily than usual, and had returned to the fields.

The female servant, Rose, remained alone in the large kitchen, where the fire on the hearth was dying out, under the large pot of hot water. From time to time she took some water out of it, and slowly washed her plates and dishes, stopping occasionally to look at the two streaks of light which the sun threw on to the long table through the window, and which showed the defects in the glass.

Three venturesome hens were picking up the crumbs under the chairs, while the smell of the poultry yard, and the warmth from the cow-stall came in through the half-open door, and a cock was heard crowing in the distance.

When she had finished her work, wiped down the table, dusted the mantel-piece, and put the plates on the high dresser, close to the wooden clock, with its sonorous ticking, she drew a long breath, as she felt rather oppressed, without exactly knowing why. She looked at the black clay walls, the rafters that were blackened with smoke, from which spiders' webs were hanging, amid red herrings and strings of onions, and then she sat down, rather overcome by the stale emanations which the floor, on which so many things had been continually spilt, gave out With this there was mingled the pungent smell of the pans of milk, which were set out to raise the cream in the adjoining dairy.

She wanted to sew, as usual, but she did not feel strong enough for it, and so she went to get a mouthful of fresh air at the door. As she felt the caressing light of the sun, her heart was filled with sweetness and a feeling of content penetrated her body.

In front of the door a shimmery haze arose from the dunghill. The fowls were lying on it; some of them were scratching with one claw in search of worms, while the cock stood up proudly among them. Every moment he selected one of them, and walked round her with a slight cluck of amorous invitation. The hen got up in a careless way as she received his attentions, bent her claws and supported him with her wings; then she shook her feathers to shake out the dust, and stretched herself out on the dunghill again, while he crowed, counting his triumphs, and the cocks in all the neighbouring farmyards replied to him, as if they were uttering amorous challenges from farm to farm.

The girl looked at them without thinking, and then she raised her eyes and was almost dazzled at the sight of the apple-trees in blossom, which looked almost like powdered heads. But just then, a colt, full of life and friskiness, galloped past her. Twice he jumped over the ditches, and then stopped suddenly, as if surprised at being alone.

She also felt inclined to run; she felt inclined to move and to stretch her limbs, and to repose in the warm, breathless air. She took a few undecided steps, and closed her eyes, for she was seized with a feeling of animal comfort; and then she went to look for the eggs in the hen loft. There were thirteen of them, which she took in and put into the sideboard; but the smell from the kitchen incommoded her again, and she went out to sit on the grass for a while.

The farmyard, which was surrounded by trees, seemed to be asleep. The tall grass, among which the yellow dandelions rose up like streaks of yellow light, was of a vivid green, fresh spring green. The apple-trees threw their shade all round them, and the thatched houses, on which the blue and yellow iris flowers with their swordlike leaves grew, smoked as if the moisture of the stables and barns were coming through the straw.

The girl went to the shed where the carts and traps were kept. Close to it, in a ditch, there was a large patch of violets, whose scent was perceptible all round, while beyond it, the open country could be seen where crops were growing, with clumps of trees in the distance, and groups of labourers here and there, who looked as small as dolls, and white horses like toys, which were pulling a child's cart, driven by a man as tall as one's finger.

She took up a bundle of straw, threw it into the ditch and sat down upon it; then, not feeling comfortable, she undid it, spread it out and lay down upon it at full length, on her back, with both arms under her head, and her legs stretched out.

Gradually her eyes closed, and she was falling into a state of delightful languor. She was, in fact, almost asleep, when she felt two hands on her bosom and then she sprang up at a bound. It was Jacques one of the farm labourers, a tall powerful fellow from Picardy, who had been making love to her for a long time. He had been looking after the sheep and seeing her lying down in the shade, he had come stealthily, holding his breath, with glistening eyes and bits of straw in his hair.

He tried to kiss her, but she gave him a smack in the face, for she was as strong as he, and he was crafty enough to beg her pardon; so they sat down side by side and talked amicably. They spoke about the weather, which was favourable for the harvest, of the season, which had begun well, of their master, who was a decent man, then of their neighbours, of all the people in the country round of themselves, of their village, of their youthful days of their recollections, of their relations, whom they would not see for a long time, perhaps never again She grew sad as she thought of it, while he, with one fixed idea in his head, rubbed against her with a kind of a shiver, overcome by desire.

"I have not seen my mother for a long time," she said. "It is very hard to be separated like that." And her gaze was lost in the distance, towards the village in the North, which she had left.

Suddenly, however, he seized her by the neck and kissed her again; but she struck him so violently in the face with her clenched fist, that his nose began to bleed, and he got up and laid his head against the trunk of a tree. When she saw that, she was sorry, and going up to him, she said: "Have I hurt you?" He, however, only laughed.

"No, it was a mere nothing;" only, she had hit him right in the middle of the nose. "What a devil!" he said, and he looked at her with admiration, for she had inspired him with a feeling of respect and of a very different kind of admiration, which was the beginning of real love for that tall, strong wench.

When the bleeding had stopped, he proposed a walk, as he was afraid of his neighbour's heavy hand, if they remained side by side like that much longer; but she took his arm of her own accord, in the avenue, as if they had been out for an evening walk, and said: "It is not nice of you to despise me like that, Jacques." He protested, however. No, he did not despise her. He was in love with her, that was all. "So you really want to marry me?" she asked.

He hesitated, and then looked at her sideways, while she looked straight ahead of her. She had fat, red cheeks, a full, protuberant bust under her loose cotton blouse, thick, red lips, and her bosom, which was almost bare, was covered with small beads of perspiration. He felt a fresh access of desire, and putting his lips to her ear, he murmured: "Yes, of course I do."

Then she threw her arms round his neck, and kissed him for such a long time that they both of them lost their breath. From that moment the eternal story of love began between them. They played with one another in corners; they met in the moonlight under a haystack, and gave each other bruises on the legs with their heavy nailed boots underneath the table. By degrees, however,

Jacques seemed to grow tired of her; he avoided her; scarcely spoke to her, and did not try any longer to meet her alone, which made her sad and anxious; and soon she found that she was pregnant.

At first, she was in a state of consternation, but then she got angry, and her rage increased every day, because she could not meet him, as he avoided her most carefully. At last, one night, when everyone in the farmhouse was asleep, she went out noiselessly in her petticoat, with bare feet, crossed the the yard and opened the door of the stable, where Jacques was lying in a large box of straw, over his horses. He pretended to snore when he heard her coming, but she knelt down by his side and shook him until he sat up.

"What do you want?" he then asked her. And she, with clenched teeth, and trembling with anger, replied: "I want . . . I want you to marry me, as you promised." But he only laughed, and replied: "Oh! If a man were to marry all the girls with whom he has made a slip, he would have more than enough to do."

Then she seized him by the throat, threw him on to his back, so that he could not disengage himself from her, and half strangling him, she shouted into his face: "I am in the family way! Do you hear? I am in the family way?"

He gasped for breath, as he was nearly choked, and so they remained, both of them, motionless and without speaking, in the dark silence, which was only broken by the noise that a horse made as he pulled the hay out of the manger, and then slowly chewed it.

When Jacques found that she was the stronger, he stammered out: "Very well, I will marry you, as that is the case." But she did not believe his promises. "It must be at once," she said. "You must have the banns put up." "At once," he replied. "Swear before God that you will." He hesitated for a few moments, and then said: "I swear it, by God."

Then she released her grasp, and went away, without another word.

She had no chance of speaking to him for several days, and as the stable was now always locked at night, she was afraid to make any noise, for fear of creating a scandal. One morning, however, she saw another man come in at dinner-time, and so she said: "Has Jacques left?" "Yes," the man replied; "I have taken his place."

This made her tremble so violently that she could not unhook the pot; and later when they were all at work, she went up into her room and cried, burying her head in her bolster, so that she might not be heard. During the day, however, she tried to obtain some information without exciting any suspicions, but she was so overwhelmed by the thoughts of her misfortune, that she fancied that all the people whom she asked, laughed maliciously. All she learned, however, was, that he had left the neighbourhood altogether.

PART II

THEN a life of constant misery began for her. She worked mechanically, without thinking of what she was doing, with one fixed idea in her head: "Suppose people were to know."

This continual feeling made her so incapable of reasoning, that she did not even try to think of any means of avoiding the disgrace that she knew must ensue, which was irreparable, and drawing nearer every day, and which was as sure as death itself. She got up every morning long before the others, and persistently tried to look at her figure in a piece of broken looking-glass at which she did her hair, as she was very anxious to know whether anybody would notice a change in her, and during the day she stopped working every few minutes to look at herself from top to toe, to see whether the size of her stomach did not make her apron look too short.

The months went on, and she scarcely spoke now, and when she was asked a question, she did not appear to understand, but she had a frightened look, with haggard eyes and trembling hands, which made her master say to her occasionly: "My poor girl, how stupid you have grown lately."

In church, she hid behind a pillar, and no longer ventured to go to confession, as she feared to face the priest, to whom she attributed superhuman powers, which enabled him to read people's consciences; and at meal times the looks of her fellow servants almost made her faint with mental agony, and she was always fancying that she had been found out by the cowherd, a precocious and cunning little lad, whose bright eyes seemed always to be watching her.

One morning the postman brought her a letter, and as she had never received one in her life before, she was so upset by it that she was obliged to sit down. Perhaps it was from him? But as she could not read, she sat anxious and trembling, with that piece of paper covered with ink in her hand; after a time, however, she put it into her pocket, as she did not venture to confide her secret to anyone. She often stopped in her work to look at those lines written at regular intervals, and which terminated in a signature, imagining vaguely that she would suddenly discover their meaning, until at last, as she felt half mad with impatience and anxiety, she went to the schoolmaster, who told her to sit down, and read to her, as follows:

"MY DEAR DAUGHTER: This is to tell you that I am very ill. Our neighbour, Monsieur Dentu, has written this letter to ask you to come, if you can. For your affectionate mother,

"CÉSAIRE DENTU,
Deputy Mayor."

She did not say a word, and went away, but as soon as she was alone, her legs gave way, and she fell down by the roadside, and remained there till night.

When she got back, she told the farmer her

trouble, who allowed her to go home for as long as she wanted, and promised to have her work done by a charwoman, and to take her back when she returned.

Her mother was dying and breathed her last the the day she arrived, and the next day Rose gave birth to a seven months' child, a miserable little skeleton, thin enough to make anybody shudder, and which seemed to be suffering continually, to judge by the painful manner in which it moved its poor little hands about, which were as thin as a crab's legs; but it lived, for all that. She said that she was married, but that she could not saddle herself with the child, so she left it with some neighbours, who promised to take care of it, and she went back to the farm.

But then, in her heart, which had been wounded so long, there arose something like brightness, an unknown love for that frail little creature which she had left behind her, but there was fresh suffering in that very love, suffering which she felt every hour and every minute, because she was parted from her child. What pained her most, however, was a mad longing to kiss it, to press it in her arms, to feel the warmth of its little body against her skin. She could not sleep at night; she thought of it the whole day long, and in the evening, when her work was done, she used to sit in front of the fire and look at it intently, like people do whose thoughts are far away.

They began to talk about her, and to tease her about the lover she must have. They asked her whether he was tall, handsome and rich. When was the wedding to be, and the christening? And often she ran away, to cry by herself, for these questions seemed to hurt her, like the prick of a pin, and in order to forget these irritations, she began to work still more energetically, and still thinking of her child, she sought for the means of saving up money for it, and determined to work so that her master would be obliged to raise her wages.

Then, by degrees, she almost monopolized the work, and persuaded him to get rid of one servant girl, who had become useless since she had taken to working like two; she saved money on the bread, oil and candles, on the corn, which they gave to the fowls too extravagantly, and on the fodder for the horses and cattle, which was rather wasted. She was as miserly about her master's money, as if it had been her own, and by dint of making good bargains, of getting high prices for all their produce, and by baffling the peasants' tricks when they offered anything for sale, he at last entrusted her with buying and selling everything, with the direction of all the labourers, and with the quantity of provisions necessary for the household, so that in a short time she became indispensable to him. She kept such a strict eye on everything about her, that under her direction the farm prospered wonderfully, and for five miles round people talked of "Master Vallin's servant," and the farmer himself said everywhere: "That girl is worth more than her weight in gold."

But time passed by, and her wages remained the same. Her hard work was accepted as something that was due from every good servant, and as a mere token of her good-will; and she began to think rather bitterly, that if the farmer could put fifty or a hundred crowns extra into the bank every month, thanks to her, she was still only earning her two hundred and forty francs a year, neither more nor less, and so she made up her mind to ask for an increase of wages. She went to see the master three times about it, but when she saw him, she spoke about something else. She felt a kind of modesty in asking for money, as if it were something disgraceful; but at last, one day, when the farmer was having breakfast by himself in the kitchen, she said to him, with some embarrassment, that she wished to speak to him particularly. He raised his head in surprise, with both his hands on the table, holding his knife, with its point in the air, in one, and a piece of bread in the other, and he looked fixedly at the girl, who felt uncomfortable under his gaze, but asked for a week's holiday, so that she might get away, as she was not very well. He acceded to her request immediately, and then added, in some embarrassment himself:

"When you come back, I shall have something to say to you, myself."

PART III

The child was nearly eight months old, and she did not know it again. It had grown rosy and chubby all over like a little bundle of living fat. She threw herself on it as if it had been some prey, and kissed it so violently that it began to scream with terror, and then she began to cry herself, because it did not know her, and stretched out its arms to its nurse, as soon as it saw her. But the next day, it began to get used to her, and laughed when it saw her, and she took it into the fields and and ran about excitedly with it, and sat down under the shade of the trees, and then, for the first time in her life, she opened her heart to somebody, and told him her troubles, how hard her work was, her anxieties and her hopes, and she quite tired the child with the violence of her caresses.

She took the greatest pleasure in handling it, in washing and dressing it, for it seemed to her that all this was the confirmation of her maternity, and she would look at it, almost feeling surprised that it was hers, and she used to say to herself in a low voice, as she danced it in her arms: "It is my baby, it is my baby."

She cried all the way home as she returned to the farm, and had scarcely got in, before her master called her into his room, and she went, feeling astonished and nervous, without knowing why.

"Sit down there," he said. She sat down, and for some moments they remained side by side, in some embarrassment, with their arms hanging at their sides, as if they did not know what to do with them, and looking each other in the face, after the manner of peasants.

The farmer, a stout, jovial, obstinate man of forty-five, who had lost two wives, evidently felt embarrassed, which was very unusual with him, but at last he made up his mind, and began to speak vaguely, hesitating a little, and looking out of the window as he talked.

"Rose," he said, "have you never thought of settling down?" She grew as pale as death, and, seeing that she gave him no answer, he went on: "You are a good, steady, active and economical girl, and a wife like you would make a man's fortune."

She did not move, but looked frightened; she did not even try to comprehend his meaning, for her thoughts were in a whirl, as if at the approach of some great danger; so after waiting for a few seconds, he went on: "You see, a farm without a mistress can never succeed, even with such a servant as you." Then he stopped, for he did not know what else to say, and Rose looked at him with the air of a person who thinks that he is face to face with a murderer, and ready to flee at the slightest movement he may make; but after waiting for about five minutes, he asked her: "Well, will it suit you?" "Will what suit me, master?" And he said, quickly: "Why, to marry me, by Jove!"

She jumped up, but fell back on to her chair as if she had been struck, and there she remained motionless, like a person who is overwhelmed by some great misfortune, but at last the farmer grew impatient, and said: "Come, what more do you want?" She looked at him almost in terror; then suddenly the tears came into her eyes, and she said twice, in a choking voice: "I cannot, I cannot!" "Why not?" he asked. "Come, don't be silly; I will give you until to-morrow to think it over."

And he hurried out of the room, very glad to have got the matter over, for it had troubled him a good deal. He had no doubt that she would the next morning accept a proposal which she could never have expected, and which would be a capital bargain for him, as he thus bound a woman to himself who would certainly bring him more than if she had the best dowry in the district.

Neither could there be any scruples about an unequal match between them, for in the country everyone is very nearly equal; the farmer works just like his labourers do, who frequently become masters in their turn, and the female servants constantly become the mistresses of the establishments, without its making any change in their lives or habits.

Rose did not go to bed that night. She threw herself, dressed as she was, on her bed, and she had not even the strength to cry left in her, she was so thoroughly overcome. She remained quite inert, scarcely knowing that she had a body, and with her mind in such a state as if it had been taken to pieces with one of those instruments which are used in re-making a mattress; only at odd moments could she collect fragments of her thoughts, and then she was frightened at the idea of what might happen. Her terror increased, and every time the great kitchen clock struck the hour she broke into a perspiration of fear. She was losing control of herself, and had a succession of nightmares; her candle went out, and then she began to imagine that some one had thrown a spell over her, like country people so often fancy, and she felt a mad inclination to run away, to escape and to flee before her misfortune, like a ship scuds before the wind.

An owl hooted, and she shivered, sat up, put her hands to her face, into her hair, and all over her body, and then she went downstairs, as if she were walking in her sleep. When she got into the yard, she stooped down, so as not to be seen by any prowling ruffian, for the moon, which was setting, shed a bright light over the fields. Instead of opening the gate, she scrambled over the bank, and as soon as she was outside, she started off. She went on straight before her, with a quick, elastic trot, and from time to time, she unconsciously uttered a piercing cry. Her long shadow accompanied her, and now and then some night bird flew over her head, while the dogs in the farmyards barked, as they heard her pass; one even jumped over the ditch and followed her and tried to bite her, but she turned round at it, and gave such a terrible yell, that the frightened animal ran back and cowered in silence in its kennel.

Sometimes a family of young hares was gambolling in a field, but when the frantic fugitive approached, like a delirious Diana, the timid creatures scampered away, the mother and her little ones disappearing into a burrow, while the father ran at full tilt, his leaping shadow, with long ears erect, standing out against the setting moon, which was now sinking down at the other end of the world, and casting an oblique light over the fields, like a huge lantern standing on the ground at the horizon.

The stars grew dim, and the birds began to twitter; day was breaking. The girl was worn out and panting, and when the sun rose in the purple sky, she stopped, for her swollen feet refused to go any farther; but she saw a pond in the distance, a large pond whose stagnant water looked like blood under the reflection of this new day, and she limped on with short steps and with her hand on her heart, in order to dip both her legs in it. She sat down on a tuft of grass, took off her heavy shoes, which were full of dust, pulled off her stockings and plunged her legs into the still water, from which bubbles were rising here and there.

A feeling of delicious coolness pervaded her from head to foot, and suddenly, while she was looking fixedly at the deep pool, she was seized with giddiness, and with a mad longing to throw herself into it. All her sufferings would be over in there; over for ever. She no longer thought of her child; she only wanted peace, complete rest, and to sleep for ever, and she got up with raised arms and took two steps forward. She was in the water up to her thighs, and she was just about to throw herself in, when sharp, pricking pains in her ankles made her jump back, and she uttered a cry of despair, for, from her knees to the tips of her feet, long, black leeches were sucking in her life blood, and were swelling, as they adhered to her flesh. She did not dare to touch them, and screamed with horror, so that her cries of despair attracted a peasant, who was driving along at some distance, to the spot. He pulled off the leeches one by one, applied herbs to the wounds, and drove the girl to her master's farm, in his gig.

She was in bed for a fortnight, and as she was sitting outside the door on the first morning that she got up, the farmer suddenly came and planted himself before her. "Well," he said, "I suppose the affair is settled, isn't it?" She did not reply at first, and then, as he remained standing and looking at her intently with his piercing eyes, she said with difficulty: "No, master, I cannot." But he immediately flew into a rage.

"You cannot, girl; you cannot? I should just like to know the reason why?" She began to cry, and repeated: "I cannot." He looked at her and then exclaimed, angrily: "Then, I suppose you have a lover?" "Perhaps that is it," she replied, trembling with shame.

The man got as red as a poppy, and stammered out in a rage: "Ah! So you confess it, you slut! And pray, who is the fellow? Some penniless, half-starved ragamuffin, without a roof to his head, I suppose? Who is it, I say?" And as she gave him no answer, he continued: "Ah! So you will not tell me. . . . Then I will tell you; it is Jean Baudu?" "No, not he," she exclaimed. "Then it is Pierre Martin?" "Oh, no, master."

And he angrily mentioned all the young fellows in the neighbourhood, while she denied that he had hit upon the right one, and every moment wiped her eyes with the corner of her big blue apron. But he still tried to find it out, with his brutish obstinacy, and, as it were, scratched her heart to discover her secret, just like a terrier scratches a hole, to try and get at the animal which he scents in it. Suddenly, however, the man shouted: "By George! It is Jacques, the man who was here last year. They used to say that you were always talking together, and that you thought about getting married."

Rose was choking, and she grew scarlet, while her tears suddenly stopped, and dried up on her cheeks, like drops of water on hot iron, and she exclaimed: "No, it is not he, it is not he!" "Is that really a fact?" the cunning peasant, who partly guessed the truth, asked; and she replied, hastily: "I will swear it; I will swear it to you . . ." She tried to think of something by which to swear, as she did not venture to invoke sacred things, but he interrupted her: "At any rate, he used to follow you into every corner, and devoured you with his eyes at meal times. Did you ever give him your promise, eh?"

This time she looked her master straight in the face. "No, never, never; I will solemnly swear to you, that if he were to come to-day and ask me to marry him, I would have nothing to do with him." She spoke with such an air of sincerity that the farmer hesitated, and then he continued, as if speaking to himself: "What, then? You have not had *a misfortune*, as they call it, or it would have been known, and as it has no consequences, no girl would refuse her master on that account. There must be something at the bottom of it, however."

She could say nothing; she had not the strength to speak, and he asked her again: "You will not?" "I cannot, master," she said, with a sigh, and he turned on his heel.

She thought she had got rid of him altogether, and spent the rest of the day almost tranquilly, but as worn out as if she had been turning the threshing machine all day, instead of the old white horse, and she went to bed as soon as she could, and fell asleep immediately. In the middle of the night, however, two hands touching the bed, woke her. She trembled with fear, but she immediately recognized the farmer's voice, when he said to her: "Don't be frightened, Rose; I have come to speak to you." She was surprised at first, but when he tried to get into the bed, she understood what he wanted, and began to tremble violently, as she felt quite alone in the darkness, still heavy from sleep, and quite naked in the bed, beside this man who desired her. She certainly did not consent, but she resisted weakly, herself struggling against that instinct which is always strong in simple natures, and very imperfectly protected, by the undecided will of inert and feeble creatures. She turned her head now to the wall, and now towards the room, in order to avoid the attentions which the farmer tried to press on her, and her body writhed a little under the coverlet, as she was weakened by the fatigue of the struggle, while he became brutal, intoxicated by desire. With a sudden movement he pulled off the bedclothes; then she saw that resistance was useless. With an ostrich-like sense of modesty she hid her face in her hands, and ceased to struggle.

They lived together as man and wife, and one morning he said to her: "I have put up our banns, and we will get married next month."

She did not reply, for what could she say? She did not resist, for what could she do?

PART IV

SHE married him. She felt as if she were in a pit vith inaccessible edges, from which she could never et out, and all kinds of misfortunes remained anging over her head, like huge rocks, which vould fall on the first occasion. Her husband gave er the impression of a man whom she had stolen, nd who would find it out some day or other. And hen she thought of her child, who was the cause of er misfortunes, but who was also the cause of all er happiness on earth, and whom she went to see wice a year, though she came back more unhappy ach time. But she gradually grew accustomed to er life, her fears were allayed, her heart was at est, and she lived with an easier mind, though till with some vague fear floating in her mind, and o years went on, and the child was six. She was lmost happy now, when suddenly the farmer's emper grew very bad.

For two or three years he seemed to have been ursing some secret anxiety, to be troubled by some are, some mental disturbance, which was gradually ncreasing. He remained at table a long time after linner, with his head in his hands, sad and devoured y sorrow. He always spoke hastily, sometimes ven brutally, and it even seemed as if he bore a grudge against his wife, for at times he answered er roughly, almost angrily.

One day, when a neighbour's boy came for some

eggs, and she spoke very crossly to him, as she was very busy, her husband suddenly came in, and said to her in his unpleasant voice: "If that were your own child you would not treat him so." She was hurt, and did not reply, and then she went back into the house, with all her grief awakened afresh, and at dinner, the farmer neither spoke to her, nor looked at her, and he seemed to hate her, to despise her, to know something about the affair at last. In consequence, she lost her head, and did not venture to remain alone with him after the meal was over, but she left the room and hastened to the church.

It was getting dusk; the narrow nave was in total darkness, but she heard footsteps in the choir, for the sacristan was preparing the tabernacle lamp for the night. That spot of trembling light, which was lost in the darkness of the arches, looked to Rose like her last hope, and with her eyes fixed on it, she fell on her knees. The chain rattled as the little lamp swung up into the air, and almost immediately the small bell rang out the *Angelus* through the increasing mist. She went up to him, as he was going out.

"Is Monsieur le Curé at home?" she asked. "Of course he is; this is his dinner-time." She trembled as she rang the bell of the priest's house. The priest was just sitting down to dinner, and he made her sit down also. "Yes, yes, I know all about it; your husband has mentioned the matter to me that brings you here." The poor woman nearly fainted, and the priest continued: "What do you want, my child?" And he hastily swallowed several spoonfuls of soup, some of which dropped on to his greasy cassock. But Rose did not venture to say anything more, and she got up to go, but the priest said: "Courage. . . ."

And she went out, and returned to the farm, without knowing what she was doing. The farmer was waiting for her, as the labourers had gone away during her absence, and she fell heavily at his feet, and shedding a flood of tears, she said to him: "What have you got against me?"

He began to shout and to swear: "What have I got against you? That I have no children, by God! When a man takes a wife, he does not want to be left alone with her until the end of his days. That is what I have against you. When a cow has no calves, she is not worth anything, and when a woman has no children, she is also not worth anything."

She began to cry, and said: "It is not my fault! It is not my fault!" He grew rather more gentle when he heard that, and added: "I do not say that it is, but it is very annoying, all the same."

PART V

FROM that day forward, she had only one thought; to have a child, another child; she confided her wish to everybody, and in consequence of this, a neighbour told her of an infallible method. This was, to make her husband a glass of water with a pinch of ashes in it, every evening. The farmer consented to try it, but without success; so they said to each other: "Perhaps there are some secret ways." And they tried to find out. They were told of a shepherd who lived ten miles off, and so Vallin one day drove off to consult him. The shepherd gave him a loaf on which he made some marks; it was kneaded up with herbs, and both of them were to eat a piece of it before and after their mutual caresses; but they ate the whole loaf without obtaining any results from it.

Next, a schoolmaster unveiled mysteries, and processes of love which were unknown in the country, but infallible, so he declared; yet none of them had the desired effect. Then the priest advised them to make a pilgrimage to the shrine at Fécamp. Rose went with the crowd and prostrated herself in the abbey, and mingling her prayers with the coarse wishes of the peasants around her, she prayed that she might be fruitful a second time; but it was in vain, and then she thought that she was being punished for her first fault, and she was seized by terrible grief. She was wasting away with sorrow; her husband was also ageing prematurely, and was wearing himself out in useless hopes.

Then war broke out between them; he called her names and beat her. They quarreled all day long, and when they were in bed together at night he flung insults and obscenities at her, panting with rage, until one night, not being able to think of any means of making her suffer more, he ordered her to get up and go and stand out of doors in the rain, until daylight. As she did not obey him, he seized her by the neck, and began to strike her in the face with his fists, but she said nothing, and did not move. In his exasperation he knelt on her stomach, and with clenched teeth, and mad with rage, he began to beat her. Then in her despair she rebelled, and flinging him against the wall with a furious gesture, she sat up, and in an altered voice, she hissed: "I have had a child, I have had one! I had it by Jacques; you know Jacques well. He promised to marry me, but he left this neighborhood without keeping his word."

The man was thunderstruck, and could hardly speak, but at last he stammered out: "What are you saying? What are you saying?" Then she began to sob, and amidst her tears she said: "That is the reason why I did not want to marry you. I could never tell you, for you would have left me without any bread for my child. You have never had any children, so you cannot understand, you cannot understand!"

He said again, mechanically, with increasing surprise: "You have a child? You have a child?"

"You had me by force, as I suppose you know? I did not want to marry you," she said, still sobbing.

Then he got up, lit the candle, and began to walk up and down, with his arms behind him. She was cowering on the bed and crying, and suddenly he stopped in front of her, and said: "Then it is my fault that you have no children?" She gave him no answer, and he began to walk up and down again, and then, stopping again, he continued: "How old is your child?" "Just six," she whispered. "Why did you not tell me about it?" he asked. "How could I?" she replied, with a sigh.

He remained standing, motionless. "Come, get up," he said. She got up, with some difficulty, and then, when she was standing on the floor, he suddenly began to laugh, with his hearty laugh of his good days, and seeing how surprised she was, he added: "Very well, we will go and fetch the child, as you and I can have none together."

She was so scared that, if she had had the strength, she would assuredly have run away, but the farmer rubbed his hands and said: "I wanted to adopt one, and now we have found one. I asked the priest about an orphan, some time ago."

Then, still laughing, he kissed his weeping and agitated wife on both cheeks, and shouted out, as if she could not hear him: "Come along, mother, we will go and see whether there is any soup left; I should not mind a plateful."

She put on her petticoat, and they went down stairs; and while she was kneeling in front of the fire-place, and lighting the fire under the pot, he continued to walk up and down the kitchen in long strides, and said:

"Well, I am really glad of this: I must say I am glad; I am really very glad."

A COUNTRY EXCURSION

FOR five months they had been talking of going to lunch at some country restaurant in the neighbourhood of Paris, on Madame Dufour's birthday, and as they were looking forward very impatiently to the outing, they had risen very early that morning. Monsieur Dufour had borrowed the milkman's cart, and drove himself. It was a very neat, two-wheeled conveyance. It had a roof supported by four iron posts to which were attached curtains, which had been raised so that they could see the countryside. The curtain at the back, alone, fluttered in the breeze like a flag. Madame Dufour, resplendent in a wonderful, cherry-coloured silk dress, sat by the side of her husband. The old grandmother and the daughter were accommodated with two chairs, and a yellow-haired youth, of whom, however, nothing was to be seen except his head, lay at the bottom of the trap.

After they had followed the Avenue des Champs-Elysées, and passed the fortifications by the Porte Maillot, they began to enjoy the scenery.

When they got to the bridge of Neuilly, Monsieur Dufour said: "Here we are in the country at last!" At that warning, his wife grew sentimental about the beauties of nature. When they got to the crossroads at Courbevoie, they were seized with admiration for the tremendous view. Down there on the right was the spire of Argenteuil church, above it rose the hills of Sannois and the mill of Orgemont, while on the left, the aqueduct of Marly stood out against the clear morning sky. In the distance they could see the terrace of Saint-Germain, and opposite to them, at the end of a low chain of hills, the new fort of Cormeilles. Far in the background, a very long way off, beyond the plains and villages, one could see the sombre green of the forests.

The sun was beginning to burn their faces, the dust got into their eyes, and on either side of the road there stretched an interminable tract of bare, ugly country, which smelled unpleasant. You would have thought that it had been ravaged by a pestilence which had even attacked the buildings, for skeletons of dilapidated and deserted houses, or small cottages left in an unfinished state, as if the contractors had not been paid, reared their four roofless walls on each side.

Here and there tall factory-chimneys rose up from the barren soil, the only vegetation on that putrid land, where the spring breezes wafted an odour of petroleum and slate, mingled with another smell that was even still less agreeable. At last, however, they crossed the Seine a second time. It was delightful on the bridge; the river sparkled in the sun, and they had a feeling of quiet satisfaction and enjoyment in drinking in purer air, not impregnated by the black smoke of factories, nor by the miasma from the dumping-grounds. A man whom they met told them that the name of the place was Bezons; so Monsieur Dufour pulled up, and read the attractive announcement outside an eating-house:

"Restaurant Poulin, fish soups and fried fish, private rooms, arbours, and swings."

"Well! Madame Dufour, will this suit you? Will you make up your mind at last?"

She read the announcement in her turn, and then looked at the house for a time.

It was a white country inn, built by the roadside, and through the open door she could see the bright zinc of the counter, at which two workmen in their Sunday best were sitting. At last she made up her mind, and said:

"Yes, this will do; and, besides, there is a view."

So they drove into a large stretch of ground planted with trees, behind the inn, which was only separated from the river by the towing-path, and got out. The husband sprang out first, and held out his arms for his wife. As the step was very high, Madame Dufour, in order to reach him, had to show the lower part of her limbs, whose former slenderness had disappeared in fat. Monsieur Dufour, who was already getting excited by the country air, pinched her calf, and then, taking her in his arms, set her on the ground, as if she had been some enormous bundle. She shook the dust out of the silk dress, and then looked round, to see in what sort of a place she was.

She was a stout woman, of about thirty-six, like a full-blown rose, and delightful to look at. She could hardly breathe, as she was laced too tightly, which forced the heaving mass of her superabundant bosom up to her double chin. Next, the girl put her hand on to her father's shoulder, and jumped lightly down. The youth with the yellow hair had got down by stepping on the wheel, and he helped Monsieur Dufour to get the grandmother out. Then they unharnessed the horse, which they tied up to a tree, and the carriage fell back, with both shafts in the air. The man and boy took off their coats, washed their hands in a pail of water, and then joined the ladies, who had already taken possession of the swings.

Mademoiselle Dufour was trying to swing herself standing up, but she could not succeed in getting a start. She was a pretty girl of about eighteen; one of those women who suddenly excite your desire when you meet them in the street, and who leave you with a vague feeling of uneasiness and of excited senses. She was tall, had a small waist and large hips, with a dark skin, very large eyes, and very black hair. Her dress clearly marked the outlines of her firm, full figure, which was accentuated by the motion of her hips as she tried to swing herself higher. Her arms were stretched over her head to hold the rope, so that her bosom rose at every movement she made. Her hat, which a gust of wind had blown off, was hanging behind her, and as the swing gradually rose higher and higher, she showed her delicate limbs up to the knees at each time, and the wind from the perfumed petticoats, more heady than the fumes of wine, blew into the faces of her father and friend, who were looking at her, smiling.

Sitting in the other swing, Madame Dufour kept saying in a monotonous voice:

"Cyprian, come and swing me; do come and swing me, Cyprian!"

At last he complied, and turning up his shirt-sleeves, as if he intended to work very hard, with much difficulty he set his wife in motion. She clutched the two ropes, and held her legs out straight, so as not to touch the ground. She enjoyed feeling giddy from the motion of the swing, and her whole figure shook like a jelly on a dish, but as she went higher and higher, she grew too giddy and got frightened. Every time she was coming back, she uttered a shriek, which made all the little urchins come round, and down below, beneath the garden hedge, she vaguely saw a row of mischievous heads, making faces as they laughed.

When a servant girl came out, they ordered lunch.

"Some fried fish, a stewed rabbit, salad, and dessert," Madame Dufour said, with an important air.

"Bring two quarts of wine, and a bottle of claret," her husband said.

"We will have lunch on the grass," the girl added.

The grandmother, who had an affection for cats, had been petting one that belonged to the house, and had been bestowing the most affectionate words on it, for the last ten minutes. The animal, no doubt secretly pleased by her attentions, kept close to the good woman, but just out of reach of her hand, and quietly walked round the trees, against which she rubbed herself, with her tail up, purring with pleasure.

"Hello!" exclaimed the youth with the yellow hair, who was ferreting about, "here are two swell boats!" They all went to look at them, and saw two beautiful skiffs in a wooden boathouse, which were as beautifully finished as if they had been objects of luxury. They were moored side by side, like two tall, slender girls, in their narrow shining length, and aroused in one a wish to drift in them on warm summer mornings and evenings, along flower-covered banks of the river, where the trees dip their branches into the water, where the rushes are continually rustling in the breeze, and where the swift kingfishers dart about like flashes of blue lightning.

The whole family looked at them with great respect.

"They are indeed two swell boats," Monsieur Dufour repeated gravely, and he examined them closely, commenting on them like a connoisseur. He had been in the habit of rowing in his younger days, he said, and when he had that in his hands — and he went through the action of pulling the oars — he did not care a fig for anybody. He had beaten more than one Englishman formerly at the Joinville regattas, and he made jokes on the word "*dames*," used to describe the two things for holding the oars. He grew quite excited at last, and offered to make a bet that in a boat like that he could row six miles an hour, without exerting himself.

"Lunch is ready," said the servant, appearing at the entrance to the boathouse. They all hurried off, but two young men were already lunching at the best place, which Madame Dufour had chosen in her mind as her seat. No doubt they were the owners of the skiffs, for they were dressed in boating costume. They were stretched out, almost lying on chairs, and were sunburned, and had on flannel trousers and thin cotton jerseys, with short sleeves, which showed their bare arms, which were as strong as blacksmiths'. They were two strong young fellows, who thought a great deal of their vigour, and who showed in all their movements that elasticity and grace of limb which can only be acquired by exercise, and which is so different from the awkwardness with which the same continual work stamps the mechanic.

They exchanged a rapid smile when they saw the mother, and then a look on seeing the daughter.

"Let us give up our place," one of them said; "it will make us acquainted with them."

The other got up immediately, and holding his black and red boating-cap in his hand, he politely offered the ladies the only shady place in the garden. With many excuses they accepted, and so that it might be more rural, they sat on the grass, without either tables or chairs.

The two young men took their plates, knives, forks, etc., to a table a little way off, and began to eat again. Their bare arms, which they showed continually, rather embarrassed the young girl, who even pretended to turn her head aside, and not to see them. But Madame Dufour, who was rather bolder, tempted by feminine curiosity, looked at them every moment, and no doubt compared them with the secret unsightliness of her husband. She had squatted herself on the ground with her legs tucked under her, after the manner of tailors, and kept wriggling about continually, under the pretext that ants were crawling about her somewhere. Monsieur Dufour, whom the presence and politeness of the strangers had put into rather a bad temper, was trying to find a comfortable position, which he did not, however, succeed in doing, while the youth with the yellow hair was eating as silently as an ogre.

"It is lovely weather, Monsieur," the stout lady said to one of the boating-men. She wished to be friendly, because they had given up their place.

"It is, indeed, Madame," he replied; "do you often go into the country?"

"Oh! Only once or twice a year, to get a little fresh air; and you, Monsieur?"

"I come and sleep here every night."

"Oh! That must be very nice?"

"Certainly it is, Madame." And he gave them such a poetical account of his daily life, that in the hearts of these shopkeepers, who were deprived of the meadows, and who longed for country walks, it roused that innate love of nature, which they all felt so strongly the whole year round, behind the counter in their shop.

The girl raised her eyes and looked at the oarsman with emotion, and Monsieur Dufour spoke for the first time.

"It is indeed a happy life," he said. And then he added: "A little more rabbit, my dear?"

"No, thank you," she replied, and turning to the young men again, and pointing to their arms, asked: "Do you never feel cold like that?"

They both laughed, and amazed the family by telling of the enormous fatigue they could endure, of bathing while in a state of tremendous perspiration, of rowing in the fog at night, and they struck their chests violently, to show how they sounded.

"Ah! You look very strong," the husband said, and he did not talk any more of the time when he used to beat the English. The girl was looking at them askance now, and the young fellow with the yellow hair, as he had swallowed some wine the wrong way, and was coughing violently, bespattered Madame Dufour's cherry-coloured silk dress. Madame got angry, and sent for some water to wash the spots.

Meanwhile it had grown unbearably hot, the sparkling river looked like a blaze of fire and the fumes of the wine were getting into their heads. Monsieur Dufour, who had a violent hiccough, had unbuttoned his waistcoat and the top of his trousers, while his wife, who felt choking, was gradually unfastening her dress. The youth was shaking his yellow mop of hair in a happy frame of mind, and kept helping himself to wine, and as the old grandmother felt drunk, she endeavoured to be very stiff and dignified. As for the girl, she showed nothing except a peculiar brightness in her eyes, while the brown skin on her cheeks became more rosy.

The coffee finished them off; they spoke of singing, and each of them sang, or repeated a couplet, which the others repeated enthusiastically. Then they got up with some difficulty, and while the two women, who were rather dizzy, were getting some fresh air, the two males, who were altogether drunk, were performing gymnastic tricks. Heavy, limp, and with scarlet faces, they hung awkwardly on to the iron rings, without being able to raise themselves while their shirts were continually threatening to part company with their trousers, and to flap in the wind like flags.

Meanwhile, the two boating-men had got their skiffs into the water. They came back, and politely asked the ladies whether they would like a row.

"Would you like one, Monsieur Dufour?" his wife exclaimed. "Please come!"

He merely gave her a drunken look, without understanding what she said. Then one of the rowers came up, with two fishing-rods in his hand; and the hope of catching a gudgeon, that great aim of the Parisian shopkeeper, made Dufour's dull eyes gleam. He politely allowed them to do whatever they liked, while he sat in the shade, under the bridge, with his feet dangling over the river, by the side of the young man with the yellow hair, who was sleeping soundly close to him.

One of the boating-men made a martyr of himself, and took the mother.

"Let us go to the little wood on the Ile aux Anglais!" he called out, as he rowed off. The other skiff went slower, for the rower was looking at his companion so intently, that he thought of nothing else. His emotion paralysed his strength, while the girl, who was sitting on the steerer's seat, gave herself up to the enjoyment of being on the water. She felt disinclined to think, felt a lassitude in her limbs, a complete self-relaxation, as if she were intoxicated. She had become very flushed, and breathed pantingly. The effect of the wine, increased by the extreme heat, made all the trees on the bank seem to bow, as she passed. A vague wish for enjoyment, a fermentation of her blood, seemed to pervade her whole body, and she was also a little agitated by this *tête-à-tête* on the water, in a place which seemed depopulated by the heat, with this young man, who thought her beautiful, whose looks seemed to caress her skin, and whose eyes were as penetrating and exciting as the sun's rays.

Their inability to speak increased their emotion, and they looked about them. At last he made an effort and asked her name.

"Henriette," she said.

"Why! My name is Henri," he replied. The sound of their voices calmed them, and they looked at the banks. The other skiff had gone ahead of them, and seemed to be waiting for them. The rower called out:

"We will meet you in the wood; we are going as far as Robinson because Madame Dufour is thirsty." Then he bent over his oars again and rowed off so quickly that he was soon out of sight.

Meanwhile, a continual roar, which they had heard for some time, came nearer, and the river itself seemed to shiver, as if the dull noise were rising from its depths.

"What is that noise?" she asked. It was the noise of the weir, which cut the river in two, at the island. He was explaining it to her, when above the noise of the waterfall they heard the song of a bird, which seemed a long way off.

"Listen!" he said; "the nightingales are singing during the day, so the females must be sitting."

A nightingale! She had never heard one before,

and the idea of listening to one roused visions of poetic tenderness in her heart. A nightingale! That is to say, the invisible witness of the lover's interview which Juliet invoked on her balcony; that celestial music which is attuned to human kisses; that eternal inspirer of all those languorous romances which open idealized visions to the poor, tender, little hearts of sensitive girls!

She was going to hear a nightingale.

"We must not make a noise," her companion said, "and then we can go into the wood, and sit down close to it."

The skiff seemed to glide. They saw the trees on the island, the banks of which were so low that they could look into the depths of the thickets. They stopped, he made the boat fast, Henriette took hold of Henri's arm, and they went beneath the trees.

"Stoop," he said, so she bent down, and they went into an inextricable thicket of creepers, leaves, and reed-grass, which formed an impenetrable retreat, and which the young man laughingly called "his private room."

Just above their heads, perched in one of the trees which hid them, the bird was still singing. He uttered shakes and trills, and then long, vibrating sounds that filled the air and seemed to lose themselves in the distance, across the level country, through that burning silence which hung low upon the whole country round. They did not speak for fear of frightening the bird away. They were sitting close together, and slowly Henri's arm stole round the girl's waist and squeezed it gently. She took that daring hand, but without anger, and kept removing it whenever he put it round her; not, however, feeling at all embarrassed by this caress, just as if it had been something quite natural which she was resisting just as naturally.

She was listening to the bird in ecstasy. She felt an infinite longing for happiness, for some sudden demonstration of tenderness, for a revelation of divine poesy. She felt such a softening at her heart, and such a relaxation of her nerves, that she began to cry, without knowing why. The young man was now straining her close to him, and she did not remove his arm; she did not think of it. Suddenly the nightingale stopped, and a voice called out in the distance:

"Henriette!"

"Do not reply," he said in a low voice, "you will drive the bird away."

But she had no idea of doing so, and they remained in the same position for some time. Madame Dufour had sat down somewhere or other, for from time to time they heard the stout lady break out into little bursts of laughter.

The girl was still crying; she was filled with delightful feelings, her skin was burning and she felt a strange sensation of tickling. Henri's head was on her shoulder, and suddenly he kissed her on the lips. She was surprised and angry, and, to avoid him, she threw herself back. But he fell upon her and his whole body covered hers. For a long time he sought her lips, which she refused him, then he pressed her mouth to his. Seized with desire she returned his kiss, holding him to her breast, and she abandoned all resistance, as if crushed by too heavy a weight.

Everything about them was still. The bird began again to sing, sending forth three penetrating notes at first, like a call of love, then, after a momentary silence, it began in weaker tones its slow modulations. A soft breeze crept up, raising a murmur among the leaves, while from the depths of the branches two burning sighs mingled with the song of the nightingale and the gentle breath of the wood.

An intoxication possessed the bird and by degrees its notes came more rapidly like a fire spreading or a passion increasing, and they seemed to be an accompaniment to the kisses which resounded beneath the tree. Then the delirium of his song burst forth. He seemed to swoon on certain notes, to have spasms of melodious emotion. Sometimes he would rest a moment, emitting only two or three slight sounds suddenly terminated on a sharp note. Or he would launch into a frenzy, pouring out his song, with thrills and jerks, like a mad song of love, followed by cries of triumph. Then he stopped, hearing beneath him a sigh so deep that it seemed as though a soul were transported. The sound was prolonged for a while, then it ended in a sob.

They were both very pale when they quitted their grassy retreat. The blue sky looked dull to them, the ardent sun was clouded over to their eyes, they perceived not the solitude and the silence. They walked quickly side by side, without speaking or touching each other, appearing to be irreconcilable enemies, as if disgust had sprung up between their bodies, and hatred between their souls. From time to time Henriette called out: "Mamma!"

They heard a noise in a thicket, and Henri fancied he saw a white dress being quickly pulled down over a fat calf. The stout lady appeared, looking rather confused, and more flushed than ever, her eyes shining and her breast heaving, and perhaps just a little too close to her companion. The latter must have had some strange experience, for his face was wrinkled with smiles that he could not check.

Madame Dufour took his arm tenderly, and they returned to the boats. Henri went on first, still without speaking, by the girl's side, and he thought he heard a loud kiss being stifled. At last they got back to Bezons.

Monsieur Dufour, who had sobered up, was waiting for them very impatiently, while the youth with the yellow hair was having a mouthful of something to eat before leaving the inn. The carriage was in the yard, with the horse yoked, and the grandmother, who had already got in, was frightened at the thought of being overtaken by night, before they got back to Paris, the outskirts not being safe.

The young men shook hands with them, and the Dufour family drove off.

"Good-bye, until we meet again!" the oarsmen cried, and the answers they got were a sigh and a tear.

. . . .

Two months later, as Henri was going along the Rue des Martyrs, he saw "Dufour, Ironmonger," over a door. So he went in, and saw the stout lady sitting at the counter. They recognized each other immediately, and after an interchange of polite greetings, he inquired after them all.

"And how is Mademoiselle Henriette?" he inquired, specially.

"Very well, thank you; she is married."

"Ah!" Mastering his feelings, he added: "To whom was she married?"

"To that young man who went with us, you know; he has joined us in business."

"I remember him perfectly."

He was going out, feeling unhappy, though scarcely knowing why, when Madame called him back.

"And how is your friend?" she asked, rather shyly.

"He is very well, thank you."

"Please give him our compliments, and beg him to come and call when he is in the neighbourhood." She blushed, then added: "Tell him it will give me great pleasure."

"I will be sure to do so. Adieu!"

"I will not say that; come again, very soon."

. . . .

The next year, one very hot Sunday, all the details of that memorable adventure suddenly came back to him so clearly that he revisited the "private room" in the wood, and was overwhelmed with astonishment when he went in. She was sitting on the grass, looking very sad, while by her side, again in his shirt-sleeves, the young man with the yellow hair was sleeping soundly, like some brute.

She grew so pale when she saw Henri, that at

first he thought she was going to faint; then, however, they began to talk quite naturally, as if there had never been anything between them. But when he told her that he was very fond of that spot, and went there very often on Sundays, to dream of old memories, she looked into his eyes for a long time. "I, too, think of it every evening," she replied.

"Come, my dear," her husband said, with a yawn; "I think it is time for us to be going."

SIMON'S FATHER

NOON had just struck. The school-door opened and the youngsters streamed out tumbling over one another in their haste to get out quickly. But instead of promptly dispersing and going home to dinner as was their daily wont, they stopped a few paces off, broke up into knots and set to whispering.

The fact was that that morning Simon, the son of La Blanchotte, had, for the first time, attended school.

They had all of them in their families heard of La Blanchotte; and although in public she was welcome enough, the mothers among themselves treated her with compassion of a somewhat disdainful kind, which the children had caught without in the least knowing why.

As for Simon himself, they did not know him, for he never went abroad, and did not play around with them through the streets of the village or along the banks of the river. So they did not like him much, and it was with a certain delight, mingled with astonishment, that they gathered in groups this morning, repeating to each other this phrase pronounced by a lad of fourteen or fifteen who appeared to know all about it, so sagaciously did he wink: "You know Simon — well, he has no father."

La Blanchotte's son appeared in his turn upon the threshold of the school.

He was seven or eight years old, rather pale, very neat, with a timid and almost awkward manner.

He was making his way back to his mother's house when the various groups of his schoolfellows, perpetually whispering, and watching him with the mischievous and heartless eyes of children bent upon playing a nasty trick, gradually surrounded him and ended by enclosing him altogether. There he stood amongst them, surprised and embarrassed, not understanding what they were going to do to him. But the lad who had brought the news, puffed up with the success he had met with, demanded:

"What is your name?"

He answered: "Simon."

"Simon what?" retorted the other.

The child, altogether bewildered, repeated: "Simon."

The lad shouted at him: "You must be named Simon something! That is not a name — Simon indeed!"

And he, on the brink of tears, replied for the third time:

"My name is Simon."

The urchins began laughing. The lad, triumphantly lifted up his voice: "You can see plainly that he has no father."

A deep silence ensued. The children were dumfounded by this extraordinary, impossibly monstrous thing — a boy who had no father; they looked upon him as a phenomenon, an unnatural being, and they felt rising in them the hitherto inexplicable pity of their mothers for La Blanchotte. As for Simon, he had propped himself against a tree to avoid falling, and he stood there as if paralysed by an irreparable disaster. He sought to explain, but he could think of no answer for them, no way to deny this horrible charge that he had no father. At last he shouted at them quite recklessly: "Yes, I have one."

"Where is he?" demanded the boy.

Simon was silent, he did not know. The children shrieked, tremendously excited. These sons of the soil, more animal than human, experienced the cruel craving which makes the fowls of a farmyard destroy one of their own kind as soon as it is wounded. Simon suddenly spied a little neighbour, the son of a widow, whom he had always seen, as he himself was to be seen, quite alone with his mother.

"And no more have you," he said, "no more have you a father."

"Yes," replied the other, "I have one."

"Where is he?" rejoined Simon.

"He is dead," declared the brat with superb dignity, "he is in the cemetery, is my father."

A murmur of approval rose amid the scapegraces, as if the fact of possessing a father dead in a cemetery made their comrade big enough to crush the other one who had no father at all. And these rogues, whose fathers were for the most part evildoers, drunkards, thieves, and harsh with their wives, hustled each other as they pressed closer and closer to Simon as though they, the legitimate ones, would stifle in their pressure one who was beyond the law.

The lad next Simon suddenly put his tongue out at him with a waggish air and shouted at him:

"No father! No father!"

Simon seized him by the hair with both hands and set to work to kick his legs while he bit his cheek ferociously. A tremendous struggle ensued. The two boys were separated and Simon found himself beaten, torn, bruised, rolled on the ground in the middle of the ring of applauding little vagabonds. As he arose, mechanically brushing his little blouse all covered with dust with his hand, some one shouted at him:

"Go and tell your father."

He then felt a great sinking in his heart. They were stronger than he, they had beaten him and he had no answer to give them, for he knew it was true that he had no father. Full of pride he tried for some moments to struggle against the tears which were suffocating him. He had a choking fit, and then without cries he began to weep with great sobs which shook him incessantly. Then a ferocious joy broke out among his enemies, and, just like savages in fearful festivals, they took one another by the hand and danced in a circle about him as they repeated in refrain:

"No father! No father!"

But suddenly Simon ceased sobbing. Frenzy overtook him. There were stones under his feet; he picked them up and with all his strength hurled them at his tormentors. Two or three were struck and ran away yelling, and so formidable did he appear that the rest became panic-stricken. Cowards, like a jeering crowd in the presence of an exasperated man, they broke up and fled. Left alone, the little thing without a father set off running toward the fields, for a recollection had been awakened which nerved his soul to a great determination. He made up his mind to drown himself in the river.

He remembered, in fact, that eight days ago a poor devil who begged for his livelihood had thrown himself into the water because he was destitute. Simon had been there when they fished him out again; and the sight of the fellow, who had seemed to him so miserable and ugly, had then impressed him — his pale cheeks, his long drenched beard, and his open eyes being full of calm. The bystanders had said:

"He is dead."

And some one had added:

"He is quite happy now."

So Simon wished to drown himself also because he had no father, just as the wretched man did who had no money.

He reached the water and watched it flowing. Some fishes were rising briskly in the clear stream and occasionally made little leaps and caught the flies on the surface. He stopped crying in order to watch them, for their feeding interested him vastly. But, at intervals, as in the lulls of a tempest, when tremendous gusts of wind snap off trees and then die away, this thought would return to him with intense pain:

"I am about to drown myself because I have no father."

It was very warm and lovely. The pleasant sunshine warmed the grass; the water shone like a mirror; and Simon enjoyed for some minutes the happiness of that languor which follows weeping, desirous even of falling asleep there upon the grass in the warmth of noon.

A little green frog leaped from under his feet. He endeavoured to catch it. It escaped him. He pursued it and lost it three times following. At last he caught it by one of its hind legs and began to laugh as he saw the efforts the creature made to escape. It gathered itself up on its large legs and then with a violent spring suddenly stretched them out as stiff as two bars. Its eyes stared wide open in their round, golden circle, and it beat the air with its front limbs, using them as though they were hands. It reminded him of a toy made with straight slips of wood nailed zigzag one on the other, which by a similar movement regulated the exercise of the little soldiers fastened thereon. Then he thought of his home and of his mother, and overcome by great sorrow he again began to weep. His limbs trembled; and he placed himself on his knees and said his prayers as before going to bed. But he was unable to finish them, for such hurried and violent sobs overtook him that he was completely overwhelmed. He thought no more, he no longer heeded anything around him but was wholly given up to tears.

Suddenly a heavy hand was placed upon his shoulder, and a rough voice asked him:

"What is it that causes you so much grief, my little man?"

Simon turned round. A tall workman, with a black beard and curly hair, was staring at him good-naturedly. He answered with his eyes and throat full of tears:

"They have beaten me because — I — I have no father — no father."

"What!" said the man smiling, "why, everybody has one."

The child answered painfully amid his spasms of grief:

"But I — I — I have none."

Then the workman became serious. He had recognized La Blanchotte's son, and although a recent arrival to the neighbourhood he had a vague idea of her history.

"Well," said he, "console yourself, my boy, and come with me home to your mother. You'll have a father."

And so they started on the way, the big one holding the little one by the hand. The man smiled again, for he was not sorry to see this Blanchotte, who by popular report was one of the prettiest girls in the country-side, and, perhaps, he said to himself at the bottom of his heart, that a lass who had erred once might very well err again.

They arrived in front of a very neat little white house.

"There it is," exclaimed the child, and he cried: "Mamma."

A woman appeared, and the workman instantly left off smiling, for he at once perceived that there was no more fooling to be done with the tall pale girl, who stood austerely at her door as though to defend from one man the threshold of that house where she had already been betrayed by another.

Intimidated, his cap in his hand, he stammered out:

"See, Madame, I have brought you back your little boy, who was lost near the river."

But Simon flung his arms about his mother's neck and told her, as he again began to cry:

"No, mamma, I wished to drown myself, because the others had beaten me — had beaten me — because I have no father."

A painful blush covered the young woman's cheeks, and, hurt to the quick, she embraced her child passionately, while the tears coursed down her face. The man, much moved, stood there, not knowing how to get away. But Simon suddenly ran up to him and said:

"Will you be my father?"

A deep silence ensued. La Blanchotte, dumb and tortured with shame, leaned against the wall, her hands upon her heart. The child, seeing that no answer was made him, replied:

"If you do not wish it, I shall return to drown myself."

The workman took the matter as a jest and answered laughing:

"Why, yes, I wish it, certainly."

"What is your name," went on the child, "so that I may tell the others when they wish to know your name?"

"Philip," answered the man.

Simon was silent a moment so that he might get the name well into his memory; then he stretched out his arms, quite consoled, and said:

"Well, then, Philip, you are my father."

The workman, lifting him from the ground kissed him hastily on both cheeks, and then strode away quickly.

When the child returned to school next day he was received with a spiteful laugh, and at the end of school, when the lad was about to begin again, Simon threw these words at his head as he would have done a stone: "My father's name is Philip."

Yells of delight burst out from all sides.

"Philip who? Philip what? What on earth is Philip? Where did you pick up your Philip?"

Simon answered nothing; and immovable in faith he defied them with his eye, ready to be martyred rather than fly before them. The schoolmaster came to his rescue and he returned home to his mother.

For about three months, the tall workman Philip, frequently passed by La Blanchotte's house and sometimes made bold to speak to her when he saw her sewing near the window. She answered him civilly, always sedately, never joking with him nor permitting him to enter her house. Notwithstanding this, being like all men, a bit of a coxcomb he imagined that she was often rosier than usual when she chatted with him.

But a fallen reputation is so difficult to recover, and always remains so fragile that, in spite of the shy reserve La Blanchotte maintained, they already gossiped in the neighbourhood.

As for Simon, he loved his new father very much, and walked with him nearly every evening when the day's work was done. He went regularly to

school and mixed in a dignified way with his school-
ellows without ever answering them back.

One day, however, the lad who had first attacked him said to him:

"You have lied. You have no father called Philip."

"Why do you say that?" demanded Simon, much disturbed.

The youth rubbed his hands. He replied:

"Because if you had one he would be your mamma's husband."

Simon was confused by the truth of this reason-
ng; nevertheless he retorted:

"He is my father all the same."

"That may well be," exclaimed the urchin with a sneer, "but that is not being your father altogether."

La Blanchotte's little one bowed his head and went off dreaming in the direction of the forge belonging to old Loizon, where Philip worked.

This forge was entombed in trees. It was very dark there, the red glare of a formidable furnace alone lit up with great flashes five blacksmiths, who hammered upon their anvils with a terrible din. Standing enveloped in flame, they worked like demons, their eyes fixed on the red-hot iron they were pounding; and their dull ideas rising and falling with their hammers.

Simon entered without being noticed and quietly plucked his friend by the sleeve. Philip turned round. All at once the work came to a standstill and the men looked on very attentively. Then, in the midst of this unaccustomed silence, rose Simon's piping voice.

"Philip, explain to me what La Michaude's boy has just told me, that you are not altogether my father."

"And why so?" asked the smith.

The child replied in all innocence:

"Because you are not my mamma's husband."

No one laughed. Philip remained standing, leaning his forehead upon the back of his great hands, which held the handle of his hammer upright upon the anvil. He mused. His four companions watched him, and, like a tiny mite among these giants, Simon anxiously waited. Suddenly, one of the smiths, voicing the sentiment of all, said to Philip:

"All the same La Blanchotte is a good and honest girl, stalwart and steady in spite of her misfortune, and one who would make a worthy wife for an honest man."

"That is true," remarked the three others.

The smith continued:

"Is it the girl's fault if she has fallen? She had been promised marriage, and I know more than one who is much respected to-day and has sinned every bit as much."

"That is true," responded the three men in chorus.

He resumed:

"How hard she has toiled, poor thing, to educate her lad all alone, and how much she has wept since she no longer goes out, save to church, God only knows."

"That is also true," said the others.

Then no more was heard save the roar of the bellows which fanned the fire of the furnace. Philip hastily bent down towards Simon:

"Go and tell your mamma that I shall come to speak to her."

Then he pushed the child out by the shoulders. He returned to his work and in unison the five hammers again fell upon their anvils. Thus they wrought the iron until nightfall, strong, powerful, happy, like Vulcans satisfied. But as the great bell of a cathedral resounds upon feast days, above the jingling of the other bells, so Philip's hammer, dominating the noise of the others, clanged second after second with a deafening uproar. His eye on the fire, he plied his trade vigorously, erect amid the sparks.

The sky was full of stars as he knocked at La Blanchotte's door. He had his Sunday blouse on, a fresh shirt, and his beard was trimmed. The young woman showed herself upon the threshold and said in a grieved tone:

"It is not right to come this way when night has fallen, Mr. Philip."

He wished to answer, but stammered and stood confused before her.

She resumed.

"And you understand quite well that it will not do that I should be talked about any more."

Then he said all at once:

"What does that matter to me, if you will be my wife!"

No voice replied to him, but he believed that he heard in the shadow of the room the sound of a body falling. He entered very quickly; and Simon, who had gone to his bed, distinguished the sound of a kiss and some words that his mother said very softly. Then he suddenly found himself lifted up by the hands of his friend, who, holding him at the length of his herculean arms, exclaimed to him:

"You will tell your school-fellows that your father is Philip Remy, the blacksmith, and that he will pull the ears of all who do you any harm."

The next day, when the school was full and lessons were about to begin, little Simon stood up quite pale with trembling lips:

"My father," said he in a clear voice, "is Philip Remy, the blacksmith, and he has promised to box the ears of all who do me any harm."

This time no one laughed any longer, for he was very well known, was Philip Remy, the blacksmith, and he was a father of whom they would all have been proud.

A FAMILY AFFAIR

THE Neuilly steam-tram had just passed the Porte Maillot, and was going along the broad avenue that terminates at the Seine. The small engine that was attached to the car whistled, to warn any obstacle to get out of its way, let off steam, panted like a person out of breath from running, and its pistons made a rapid noise, like iron legs running. The oppressive heat of the end of a summer day lay over the whole city, and from the road, although there was not a breath of wind stirring, there arose a white, chalky, opaque, suffocating, and warm dust which stuck to the moist skin, filled the eyes, and got into the lungs. People were standing in the doors of their houses in search of a little air.

The windows of the steam-tram were down, and the curtains fluttered in the wind. There were very few passengers inside, because on such warm days people preferred the top or the platforms. The few inside consisted of stout women in strange toilettes, shopkeepers' wives from the suburbs, who made up for the distinguished looks which they did not possess by ill-assumed dignity; of gentlemen tired of their office, with yellow faces, who stooped with one shoulder higher than the other, in consequence of long hours of work bending over the desk. Their uneasy and melancholy faces also spoke of domestic troubles, of constant want of money, of former hopes that had been finally disappointed. They all belonged to that army of poor, threadbare devils who vegetate economically in mean, plastered houses, with a tiny grass border for a garden, in the midst of the district where rubbish is deposited, on the outskirts of Paris.

Near the door a short, fat man, with a puffy face and a big stomach, dressed in black and wearing a decoration in his buttonhole, was talking to a tall, thin man, attired in a dirty, white linen suit all unbuttoned, and wearing a white Panama hat. The former spoke so slowly and hesitatingly, that occasionally it almost seemed as if he stammered; it was Monsieur Caravan, chief clerk in the Admiralty. The other, who had formerly been surgeon on board a merchant ship, had set up in practice in Courbevoie, where he applied the vague remnants of medical knowledge which he had retained after an adventurous life, to healing the wretched population of that district. His name was Chenet, and he had made the people call him Doctor, and strange rumours were current as to his morality.

Monsieur Caravan had always led the normal life of a man in a government office. Every morning for the last thirty years he had invariably gone the same way to his office, had met the same men going to business at the same time and nearly on the same spot, returned home every evening the same way, and again met the same faces, which he had seen growing old. Every morning, after buying his half-penny paper at the corner of the Faubourg

Saint-Honoré, he bought his two rolls, and then rushed to his office, like a culprit giving himself up to justice. He got to his desk as quickly as possible, always feeling uneasy, as if expecting a rebuke for some neglect of duty of which he might have been guilty.

Nothing had ever occurred to change the monotonous order of his existence; no event affected him except the work of his office, gratuities, and promotion. He never spoke of anything but of his duties, either at the Admiralty or at home, for he had married the portionless daughter of one of his colleagues. His mind, which was in a state of atrophy from his depressing daily work, had no other thoughts, hopes, or dreams than such as related to the office, and there was a constant source of bitterness that spoiled every pleasure that he might have had, and that was the employment of so many commissioners of the navy, "tinmen," as they were called, because of their silver-lace, as first-class clerks and heads of departments. Every evening at dinner he discussed the matter hotly with his wife, who shared his angry feelings, and proved to their own satisfaction that it was in every way unjust to give jobs in Paris to men who ought properly to have been employed in the navy.

He was old now, and had scarcely noticed how his life was passing, for school had merely been exchanged, without any transition, for the office, and the ushers at whom he had formerly trembled were replaced by his chiefs, of whom he was terribly afraid. When he had to go into the rooms of these official despots, it made him tremble from head to foot, and that constant fear had given him a very awkward manner in their presence, a humble demeanour, and a kind of nervous stammering.

He knew nothing more about Paris than a blind man could know, who was led to the same spot by his dog every day. If he read the account of any uncommon events, or of scandals, in his half-penny paper, they appeared to him like fantastic tales, which some pressman had made up out of his own head, in order to amuse minor clerks. He did not read the political news, which his paper frequently altered, as the cause which subsidized them might require, for he was not fond of innovations, and when he went through the Avenue of the Champs-Elysées every evening, he looked at the surging crowd of pedestrians, and at the stream of carriages, like a traveller who has lost his way in a strange country.

As he had completed his thirty years of obligatory service that year, on the first of January, he had had the cross of the Legion of Honour bestowed upon him, which, in the semi-military public offices, is a recompense for the long and miserable slavery — the official phrase is, "loyal services" — of unfortunate convicts who are riveted to their desks. That unexpected dignity gave him a high and new idea of his own capacities, and altogether altered him. He immediately left off wearing light trousers and fancy waistcoats, and wore black trousers and long coats, on which his "ribbon," which was very broad, showed off better. He got shaved every morning, trimmed his nails more carefully, changed his linen every two days, from a legitimate sense of what was proper, and out of respect for the national Order of which he formed a part. In fact, from that day he was another Caravan, scrupulously clean, majestic, and condescending.

At home, he said, "my cross," at every moment, and he had become so proud of it that he could not bear to see other men wearing any other ribbon in their buttonholes. He got angry when he saw strange orders, which "nobody ought to be allowed to wear in France," and he bore Chenet a particular grudge, as he met him on a tram-car every evening, wearing a decoration of some sort or another, white, blue, orange, or green.

The conversation of the two men, from the Arc de Triomphe to Neuilly, was always the same. That day as usual, they discussed, first of all, various local abuses, which disgusted them both, and the mayor of Neuilly received his full share of the blame. Then, as invariably happens in the company of a medical man, Caravan began to enlarge on the subject of illness, as, in that manner, he hoped to obtain a little gratuitous advice, or even a consultation if he were careful enough not to give himself away. His mother had been causing him no little anxiety for some time; she had frequent and prolonged fainting fits, and, although she was ninety, she would not take care of herself.

Caravan grew quite tender-hearted when he mentioned her great age, and more than once asked Doctor Chenet, emphasizing the word "doctor," whether he had often met anyone as old as that. And he rubbed his hands with pleasure; not, perhaps, that he cared very much about seeing the good woman last forever here on earth, but because the long duration of his mother's life was, as it were, an earnest of old age for himself. Then he continued:

"In my family, we last long, and I am sure that, unless I meet with an accident, I shall not die until I am very old."

The officer of health looked at him with pity, glancing for a moment at his neighbour's red face, his short, thick neck, his "corporation," as Chenet called it, that hung down between two flaccid, fat legs, and the apoplectic rotundity of the old, flabby official. Lifting the dirty Panama hat which he wore from his head, he said, with a snigger:

"I am not so sure of that, old fellow; your mother is as tough as nails, and I should say that your life is not a very good one."

This rather upset Caravan, who did not speak again until the tram put them down at their destination. The two friends got out, and Chenet asked his friend to have a glass of vermouth at the Café du Globe, opposite, a place which both of them were in the habit of frequenting. The proprietor, who was a friend of theirs, held out two fingers to them, which they shook across the bottles on the counter, and then they joined three of their friends, who were playing at dominoes, and had been there since midday. They exchanged cordial greetings, with the usual inquiry: "Anything fresh?" Then the three players continued their game, and held out their hands without looking up, when the others wished them "Good night" and went home to dinner.

Caravan lived in a small, two-storied house in Courbevoie, near the meeting of the roads; the ground floor was occupied by a hairdresser. Two bedrooms, a dining-room, and a kitchen where mended chairs wandered from room to room, as they were wanted, formed the whole of their apartments, and Madame Caravan spent nearly her whole time in cleaning them up, while her daughter, Marie-Louise, who was twelve, and her son, Philippe-Auguste, were running about with all the little, dirty, mischievous brats of the neighbourhood, and playing in the gutters.

Caravan had installed his mother, whose avarice was notorious in the neighbourhood, and who was terribly thin, in the room above them. She was always in a bad temper and never passed a day without quarrelling and flying into furious tempers. She used to apostrophise the neighbours standing at their own doors, the vegetable venders, the street-sweepers, and the street-boys, in the most violent language. The latter, to have their revenge, used to follow her at a distance when she went out and call out rude things after her.

A little servant from Normandy, who was incredibly giddy and thoughtless, performed the household work, and slept on the second floor in the same room as the old woman, for fear of anything happening to her in the night.

When Caravan got in, his wife, who suffered from a chronic passion for cleaning, was polishing up the mahogany chairs, that were scattered about the room, with a piece of flannel. She always wore cotton gloves and adorned her head with a cap, ornamented with many coloured ribbons, which was always tilted on one ear, and whenever anyone caught her, polishing, sweeping, or washing, she used to say:

"I am not rich; everything is very simple in my house, but cleanliness is my luxury, and that is worth quite as much as any other."

As she was gifted with sound, obstinate, practical common sense, she swayed her husband in everything. Every evening during dinner, and afterward, when they were in bed, they talked over the business in the office, and, although she was twenty years younger, he confided everything to her as if she had had the direction, and followed her advice in every matter.

She had never been pretty, and now had grown ugly; in addition to that, she was short and thin, while her careless and tasteless way of dressing herself hid the few, small feminine attributes which might have been brought out if she had possessed any skill in dress. Her petticoats were always awry, and she frequently scratched herself, no matter on what place, totally indifferent as to who might be there, out of a sort of habit which had become almost an unconscious movement. The only ornaments that she allowed herself were silk ribbons, which she had in great profusion, and of various colours mixed together, in the pretentious caps which she wore at home.

As soon as she saw her husband she got up, and said, as she kissed him:

"Did you remember Potin, my dear?"

He fell into a chair, in consternation, for that was the fourth time he had forgotten a commission that he had promised to do for her.

"It is a fatality," he said; "in spite of my thinking of it all day long, I am sure to forget it in the evening."

But as he seemed really so very sorry, she merely said, quietly:

"You will think of it to-morrow, I daresay. Anything fresh at the office?"

"Yes, a great piece of news: another tinman has been appointed senior chief clerk." She became angry.

"To what department?"

"The department of Foreign Supplies."

"So he succeeds Ramon. That was the very post that I wanted you to have. And what about Ramon?"

"He retires on his pension."

She grew furious, her cap slid down on her shoulder, and she continued:

"There is nothing more to be done in that hole now. And what is the name of the new commissioner?"

"Bonassot."

She took up the "Naval Year Book," which she always kept close at hand, and looked him up:

"'Bonassot — Toulon. Born in 1851. Student-Commissioner in 1871. Sub-Commissioner in 1875.'

Has he been to sea?" she continued, and at that question Caravan's looks cleared up, and he laughed until his sides shook.

"Just like Balin — just like Balin, his chief." Then he added an old office joke, and laughed more than ever:

"It would not even do to send them by water to inspect the Point-du-Four, for they would be sick on the Seine steamboats."

But she remained as serious as if she had not heard him, and then she said in a low voice, while she scratched her chin:

"If only we had a deputy to fall back upon. When the Chamber hears all that is going on at the Admiralty, the minister will be turned out —"

She was interrupted by a terrible noise on the stairs. Marie-Louise and Philippe-Auguste, who had just come in from the gutter, were giving each other slaps all the way upstairs. Their mother rushed at them furiously, and taking each of them by an arm, she dragged them into the room, shaking them vigorously. But as soon as they saw their father, they rushed up to him. He kissed them affectionately, and taking one of them on each knee, he began to talk to them.

Philippe-Auguste was an ugly, ill-kempt little brat, dirty from head to foot, with the face of an idiot, and Marie-Louise was already like her mother — spoke like her, repeated her words, and even imitated her movements. She also asked him whether there was anything fresh at the office, and he replied merrily:

"Your friend, Ramon, who comes and dines here every Sunday, is going to leave us, little one. There is a new senior head-clerk."

She looked at her father, and with a precocious child's pity, she said:

"So somebody has been put over your head again!"

He stopped laughing and did not reply. Then, in order to create a diversion, he said, addressing his wife, who was cleaning the windows:

"How is mamma, up there?"

Madame Caravan left off rubbing, turned round, pulled her cap up, as it had fallen quite on to her back, and said, with trembling lips:

"Ah! yes; let us talk about your mother. She has created a pretty scene. Just think that a short time ago Madame Lebaudin, the hairdresser's wife, came upstairs to borrow a packet of starch from me, and, as I was not at home, your mother called her *a beggar woman*, and turned her out; but I gave it to the old woman. She pretended not to hear, as she always does when one tells her unpleasant truths, but she is no more deaf than I am, as you know. It is all a sham, and the proof of it is, that she went up to her own room immediately without saying a word."

Caravan, taken aback, did not utter a word, and at that moment the little servant came in to announce dinner. In order to let his mother know, he took a broom-handle, which always stood hidden in a corner, and rapped loudly on the ceiling three times, and then they went into the dining-room. Madame Caravan, junior, helped the soup, and waited for the old woman. But she did not come, and the soup was getting cold, so they began to eat slowly, and when their plates were empty, they waited again. Then Madame Caravan, who was furious, attacked her husband:

"She does it on purpose, you know that as well as I do. But you always uphold her."

In great perplexity between the two, he sent up Marie-Louise to fetch her grandmother, and sat motionless, with his eyes down, while his wife tapped her glass angrily with her knife. In about a minute the door flew open suddenly, and the child came in again, out of breath, and very pale, and said quickly:

"Grandmamma has fallen down on the ground."

Caravan jumped up, threw his table-napkin down, and rushed upstairs, while his wife, who thought it was some trick of her mother-in-law, followed more slowly, shrugging her shoulders, as if to express her doubt. When they got upstairs, however, they found the old woman lying at full length in the middle of the room, and when they turned her over they saw that she was insensible and motionless. Her skin looked more wrinkled and yellow than usual, her eyes were closed, her teeth clenched, and her thin body was stiff.

Caravan kneeled down by her and began to moan:

"My poor mother! my poor mother!" he said. But the other Madame Caravan said:

"Bah! She has only fainted again, that is all, and she has done it to prevent us from dining comfortably, you may be sure of that."

They put her on the bed, undressed her completely, and Caravan, his wife, and the servant began to rub her, but, in spite of their efforts, she did not recover consciousness, so they sent Rosalie, the servant, to fetch "Doctor" Chenet. He lived a long way off, on the quay going toward Suresnes, and so it was a considerable time before he arrived. He came at last, however, and, after having looked at the old woman, felt her pulse, and auscultated her, he said:

"It is all over."

Caravan threw himself on the body, sobbing violently. He kissed his mother's rigid face, and wept so that great tears fell on the dead woman's face, like drops of water. Naturally, Madame Caravan, junior, showed a decorous amount of grief, uttered feeble moans as she stood behind her husband, and she rubbed her eyes vigorously.

But, suddenly, Caravan raised himself up, with his thin hair in disorder, and, looking very ugly in his grief, said:

"But, are you sure, doctor? Are you quite sure?"

The medical man stooped over the body, and, handling it with professional dexterity, as a shopkeeper might do, when showing off his goods, he said: "See, my dear friend, look at her eye."

He raised the eyelid and the old woman's look reappeared under his finger, altogether unaltered, unless, perhaps, the pupil was rather larger, and Caravan felt a severe shock at the sight. Then Monsieur Chenet took her thin arm, forced the fingers open, and said, angrily, as if he had been contradicted:

"Just look at her hand; I never make a mistake, you may be quite sure of that."

Caravan fell on the bed, and almost bellowed, while his wife, still whimpering, did what was necessary.

She brought the night-table, on which she spread a table-napkin. Then she placed four wax candles on it, which she lighted; then took a sprig of box, which was hanging over the chimney glass, and put it between the candles, into the plate, which she filled with clean water, as she had no holy water. After a moment's rapid reflection, she threw a pinch of salt into the water, no doubt thinking she was performing some sort of act of consecration by doing that. When she had finished the setting which is supposed to be appropriate to Death, she remained standing motionless, and the medical man, who had been helping her, whispered to her:

"We must take Caravan away."

She nodded assent, and, going up to her husband, who was still on his knees, sobbing, she raised him up by one arm, while Chenet took him by the other.

They put him into a chair, and his wife kissed his forehead and then began to lecture him. Chenet enforced her words, and preached firmness, courage, and resignation — the very things which are always wanting in such overwhelming misfortune — and then both of them took him by the arms again and led him out.

He was crying like a big child, with convulsive sobs; his arms were hanging down and his legs seemed useless; he went downstairs without knowing what he was doing, and moved his legs mechanically. They put him into the chair which he always occupied at dinner, in front of his empty soup-plate. And there he sat, without moving, with his eyes fixed on his glass, so stupefied with grief that he could not even think.

In a corner, Madame Caravan was talking with the doctor, and asking what the necessary formalities were, as she wanted to obtain practical information. At last, Monsieur Chenet, who appeared to be waiting for something, took up his hat and prepared to go, saying that he had not dined yet; whereupon she exclaimed:

"What! You have not dined? But stop here, doctor; don't go. You shall have whatever we can give you, for, of course, you will understand that we won't eat much." However, he made excuses and refused, but she persisted, and said:

"You really must stop; at times like this people like to have friends near them, and, besides that, perhaps you will be able to persuade my husband to take some nourishment; he must keep up his strength."

The doctor bowed, and, putting down his hat, said:

"In that case, I will accept your invitation, Madame."

She gave Rosalie, who seemed to have lost her head, some orders, and then sat down, "to pretend to eat," as she said, "to keep the 'doctor' company."

The soup was brought in again, and Monsieur Chenet took two helpings. Then there came a dish of tripe, which exhaled a smell of onions, and which Madame Caravan made up her mind to taste.

"It is excellent," the doctor said, at which she smiled, and, turning to her husband, she said:

"Do take a little, my poor Alfred, only just to get something into your stomach. Remember that you have got to pass the night watching by her!"

He held out his plate, docilely, just as he would have gone to bed if he had been told to, obeying her in everything without resistance and without reflection, and, therefore, he ate. The doctor helped himself three times, while Madame Caravan, from time to time, fished out a large piece on the end of her fork, and swallowed it with a sort of studied inattention.

When a salad bowl full of macaroni was brought in, the doctor said:

"By Jove! That is what I am very fond of." And this time Madame Caravan helped everybody. She even filled the children's saucers, which they had scraped clean, and who, being left to themselves, had been drinking wine without any water, and were now kicking each other under the table.

Chenet remembered that Rossini, the composer, had been very fond of that Italian dish, and suddenly he exclaimed:

"Why! that rhymes, and one could begin some lines like this:

"The Maestro Rossini
Was fond of macaroni."

Nobody listened to him, however. Madame Caravan, who had suddenly grown thoughtful, was thinking of all the probable consequences of the event, while her husband made bread pellets, which he put on the table-cloth, and looked at with a fixed, idiotic stare. As he was devoured by thirst, he was continually raising his glass to his lips, and the consequence was that his senses, already rather upset by the shock and grief, seemed to dance about vaguely in his head, which was heavy from the laborious process of digestion which had begun.

Meanwhile, the doctor, who had been drinking away steadily, was getting visibly drunk, and Madame Caravan herself felt the reaction which follows all nervous shocks. She was agitated and excited, and although she had been drinking nothing but water, she felt her head rather confused.

By and by, Chenet began to relate stories of deaths, that appeared funny to him. In the suburbs of Paris, which are full of people from the provinces, one meets with the indifference toward death, even of a father or a mother, which all peasants show; a want of respect, an unconscious callousness which is common in the country, and rare in Paris. Said he:

"Why, I was sent for last week to the Rue du Puteaux, and when I went, I found the sick person (and there was the whole family calmly sitting near the bed) finishing a bottle of liqueur of aniseed, which had been bought the night before to satisfy the dying man's fancy."

But Madame Caravan was not listening; she was continually thinking of the inheritance, and Caravan was incapable of understanding anything.

Soon Rosalie served coffee, which had been made very strong, to keep up their courage, and as every cup was well dosed with cognac, it made all their faces red, and confused their ideas still more. To make matters still worse, Chenet suddenly seized the brandy bottle and poured out "a drop just to wash their mouths out with," as he termed it, for each of them. Then, without speaking any more, overcome, in spite of themselves, by that feeling of animal comfort which alcohol affords after dinner, they slowly sipped the sweet cognac, which formed a yellowish syrup at the bottom of their cups.

The children had gone to sleep, and Rosalie carried them off to bed. Then, Caravan, mechanically obeying that wish to forget oneself which possesses all unhappy persons, helped himself to brandy again several times, and his dull eyes grew bright. At last the doctor rose to go, and seizing his friend's arm, he said:

"Come with me; a little fresh air will do you good. When you are in trouble, you must not stick to one spot."

The other obeyed mechanically, put on his hat, took his stick, and went out, and both of them went arm-in-arm toward the Seine, in the starlight night.

The air was warm and sweet, for all the gardens in the neighbourhood are full of flowers at that season of the year, and their scent, which is scarcely perceptible during the day, seems to awaken at the approach of night, and mingles with the light breezes which blow upon them in the darkness.

The broad avenue, with its two rows of gas-lamps, which extend as far as the Arc de Triomphe, was deserted and silent, but there was the distant roar of Paris, which seemed to have a reddish vapour hanging over it. It was a kind of continual rumbling, which was at times answered by the whistle of a train at full speed, in the distance, travelling to the ocean through the provinces.

The fresh air on the faces of the two men rather overcame them at first, made the doctor lose his equilibrium a little, and increased Caravan's giddiness, from which he had suffered since dinner. He walked as if he were in a dream; his thoughts were paralysed; although he felt no great grief, for he was in a state of mental torpor that prevented him from suffering, and he even felt a sense of relief which was increased by the warm scent of the night.

When they reached the bridge, they turned to the right and faced the fresh breeze from the river, which rolled along, calm and melancholy, bordered by tall poplar-trees. The stars looked as if they were floating on the water and were moving with the current. A slight, white mist that floated over the opposite banks filled their lungs with a sensation of cold, and Caravan stopped suddenly, for he was struck by that smell from the water, which brought back old memories to his mind. For suddenly, in his mind, he saw his mother again, in Picardy, as he had seen her years before, kneeling in front of their door and washing the heaps of linen, by her side, in the little stream that ran through their garden. He almost fancied that he could hear the sound of the wooden beetle with which she beat the linen, in the calm silence of the country, and her voice, as she called out to him: "Alfred, bring me some soap." And he smelled the odour of the trickling water, of the mist rising from the wet ground, of the heap of wet linen which he should never forget, the less that it came back to him on the very evening on which his mother died.

He stopped, paralysed by a sudden feeling of anguish. It was like a beam of light illuminating all at once the whole extent of his misfortune, and this meeting with vagrant thoughts plunged him into a black abyss of irremediable despair. He felt heartbroken at that eternal separation. His life seemed cut in half, all his youth gone, swallowed up by that death. All the *former* life was over and done with, all the recollections of his youthful days would vanish; for the future, there would be nobody to talk to him of what had happened in days gone by, of the people he had known of old, of his own part of the country, and of his past life; that was a part of his existence which was gone forever, and the other might as well end now.

Then the procession of memories came. He saw his mother as she was when younger, wearing well-worn dresses, which he remembered for such a long time that they seemed inseparable from her. He recollected her in various forgotten circumstances, her suppressed appearance, the different tones of her voice, her habits, her manias, her fits of anger, the wrinkles on her face, the movements of her thin fingers, and all her well-known attitudes, which she would never have again, and clutching hold of the doctor, he began to moan and weep. His flabby legs began to tremble, his whole stout body was shaken by his sobs, all he could say was:

"My mother, my poor mother, my poor mother!"

But his companion, who was still drunk, and who intended to finish the evening in certain places of bad repute that he frequented secretly, made him sit down on the grass by the riverside, and left him almost immediately, under the pretext that he had to see a patient.

Caravan went on crying for a long time, and then, when he had got to the end of his tears — when his grief had, so to speak, run out of him — he again felt relief, repose, and sudden tranquillity.

The moon had risen and bathed the horizon in its soft light. The tall poplar-trees had a silvery sheen on them, and the mist on the plain looked like floating snow. The river, in which the stars were no longer reflected, and which looked as if it were covered with mother-of-pearl, flowed on, rippled by the wind. The air was soft and sweet, and Caravan inhaled it almost greedily, thinking that he could perceive a feeling of freshness, of calm and of superhuman consolation pervading him.

He really tried to resist that feeling of comfort and relief, and kept on saying to himself: "My mother, my poor mother!" He tried to make himself cry, from a kind of conscientious feeling, but he could not succeed in doing so any longer, and the sad thoughts which had made him sob so bitterly a short time before had almost passed away. In a few moments he rose to go home, and returned slowly, under the influence of that serene night, with a heart soothed in spite of himself.

When he reached the bridge, he saw the last tram-car, ready to start, and the lights through the windows of the Café du Globe, and felt a longing to tell somebody of the catastrophe that had happened, to excite pity, to make himself interesting. He put on a woeful face, pushed open the door, and went up to the counter, where the landlord always stood. He had counted on creating an effect, and had hoped that everybody would get up and come to him with outstretched hands, and say: "Why, what is the matter with you?" But nobody noticed his disconsolate face, so he rested his two elbows on the counter, and, burying his face in his hands, he murmured: "Good heavens! Good heavens!"

The landlord looked at him and said: "Are you ill, Monsieur Caravan?"

"No, my friend," he replied, "but my mother has just died."

"Ah!" the other exclaimed, and as a customer at the other end of the establishment asked for a glass of beer, he replied: "All right, I'm coming," and he went to attend to him, leaving Caravan almost stupefied at his want of sympathy.

The three domino players were sitting at the same table which they had occupied before dinner, totally absorbed in their game, and Caravan went up to them, in search of pity, but as none of them appeared to notice him, he made up his mind to speak.

"A great misfortune has happened to me since I was here," he said.

All three raised their heads slightly at the same instant, but kept their eyes fixed on the pieces which they held in their hands.

"What do you say?"

"My mother has just died."

Whereupon one of them said: "Oh! By Jove!" with that false air of sorrow which indifferent people assume. Another, who could not find anything to say, emitted a sort of sympathetic whistle, shaking his head at the same time, and the third turned to the game again, as if he were saying to himself: "Is that all!"

Caravan had expected some of those expressions that are said to "come from the heart," and when he saw how his news was received he left the table, indignant at their calmness before a friend's sorrow, although at that moment he was so dazed with grief that he hardly felt it, and went home.

His wife was waiting for him in her nightgown, sitting in a low chair by the open window, still thinking of the inheritance.

"Undress yourself," she said; "we will talk when we are in bed."

He raised his head, and looking at the ceiling, he said:

"But there is nobody up there."

"I beg your pardon, Rosalie is with her, and you can go and take her place at three o'clock in the morning, when you have had some sleep."

He only partially undressed, however, so as to be ready for anything that might happen, and after tying a silk handkerchief round his head, he joined his wife, who had just got in between the sheets. For some time they remained side by side, and neither of them spoke. She was thinking.

Even in bed, her nightcap was adorned with a pink bow, and was pushed rather over one ear, as was the way with all the caps that she wore. Presently, she turned toward him and said:

"Do you know whether your mother made a will?"

He hesitated for a moment, and then replied:

"I — I do not think so. No, I am sure that she did not."

His wife looked at him, and she said, in a low, furious voice:

"I call that infamous; here we have been wearing ourselves out for ten years in looking after her, and have boarded and lodged her! Your sister would not have done so much for her, nor I either, if I had known how I was to be rewarded! Yes, it is a disgrace to her memory! I daresay that you will tell me that she paid us, but one cannot pay one's children in ready money for what they do; that obligation is recognized after death; at any rate, that is how honourable people act. So I have had all my worry and trouble for nothing! Oh, that is nice! that is very nice!"

Poor Caravan, who felt nearly distracted, kept on saying:

"My dear, my dear, please, please be quiet."

She grew calmer by degrees, and, resuming her usual voice and manner, she continued:

"We must let your sister know to-morrow."

He started, and said:

"Of course we must; I had forgotten all about it; I will send her a telegram the first thing in the morning."

"No," she replied, like a woman who has foreseen everything; "no, do not send it before ten or eleven o'clock, so that we may have time to turn round before she comes. It does not take more than two hours to get here from Charenton, and we can say that you lost your head from grief. If we let her know in the course of the day, that will be soon enough, and will give us time to look round."

But Caravan put his hand to his forehead, and in the same timid voice in which he always spoke of his chief, the very thought of whom made him tremble, he said:

"I must let them know at the office."

"Why?" she replied. "On such occasions like this, it is always excusable to forget. Take my advice, and don't let him know; your chief will not be able to say anything to you, and you will put him into a nice fix."

"Oh! yes, I shall, indeed, and he will be in a terrible rage, too, when he notices my absence. Yes, you are right; it is a capital idea, and when I tell him that my mother is dead, he will be obliged to hold his tongue."

And he rubbed his hands in delight at the joke, when he thought of his chief's face; while the body of the dead old woman lay upstairs, beside the sleeping servant.

But Madame Caravan grew thoughtful, as if she were preoccupied by something which she did not care to mention. But at last she said:

"Your mother had given you her clock, had she not; the girl playing at cup and ball?"

He thought for a moment, and then replied:

"Yes, yes; she said to me a long time ago, when

she first came here: 'I shall leave the clock to you, if you look after me well.'"

Madame Caravan was reassured, and regained her serenity, and said:

"Well, then, you must go and fetch it out of her room, for if we get your sister here, she will prevent us from having it."

He hesitated: "Do you think so?" That made her angry.

"I certainly think so; as soon as it is in our possession, she will know nothing at all about where it came from; it belongs to us. It is just the same with the chest of drawers with the marble top that is in her room; she gave it to me one day when she was in a good temper. We will bring it down at the same time."

Caravan, however, seemed incredulous, and said:

"But, my dear, it is a great responsibility!"

She turned on him furiously.

"Oh! Indeed! Will you never alter? You would let your children die of hunger, rather than make a move. Does not that chest of drawers belong to us, since she gave it to me? And if your sister is not satisfied, let her tell me so, me! I don't care a straw for your sister. Come, get up, and we will bring down what your mother gave us, immediately."

Trembling and vanquished, he got out of bed, and began to put on his trousers, but she stopped him:

"It is not worth while to dress yourself; your underclothes are quite enough; I mean to go as I am."

They both left the room in their nightclothes, went upstairs quite noiselessly, opened the door, and went into the room where the four lighted tapers and the plate with the sprig of box alone seemed to be watching the old woman in her rigid repose; for Rosalie, who was lying back in the easy-chair with her legs stretched out, her hands folded in her lap, and her head on one side, was also quite motionless, and snoring with her mouth wide open.

Caravan took the clock, which was one of those grotesque objects that were produced so plentifully under the Empire. A girl in gilt bronze was holding a cup and ball, and the ball formed the pendulum.

"Give that to me," his wife said, "and take the marble top off the chest of drawers."

He put the marble on his shoulder with a considerable effort, and they left the room. Caravan had to stoop in the doorway, and trembled as he went downstairs, while his wife walked backward, so as to light him, holding the candlestick in one hand and the clock under her other arm.

When they were in their own room, she heaved a sigh.

"We have got over the worst part of the job," she said; "so now let us go and fetch the other things."

But the drawers were full of the old woman's wearing apparel which they must manage to hide somewhere, and Madame Caravan soon thought of a plan.

"Go and get that wooden box in the passage; it is hardly worth anything and we may just as well put it here."

And when he had brought it upstairs, the change began. One by one, she took out all the collars, cuffs, chemises, caps, all the well-worn things that had belonged to the poor woman lying there behind them, and arranged them methodically in the wooden box, in such a manner as to deceive Madame Braux, the deceased woman's other child, who would be coming the next day.

When they had finished, they first of all carried the drawers downstairs, and the remaining portion afterward, each of them holding an end. It was some time before they could make up their minds where it would stand best; but at last they settled upon their own room, opposite the bed, between the two windows. As soon as it was in its place, Madame Caravan filled it with her own things. The clock was placed on the chimney-piece in the dining-room. They looked to see what the effect was, and were both delighted with it, agreeing that nothing could be better. Then they got into bed, she blew out the candle, and soon everybody in the house was asleep.

It was broad daylight when Caravan opened his eyes again. His mind was rather confused when he woke up, and he did not clearly remember what had happened for a few minutes; when he did, he felt it painfully, and jumped out of bed, almost ready to cry again.

He very soon went to the room overhead, where Rosalie was still sleeping in the same position as the night before, for she did not wake up once during the whole time. He sent her to do her work, put fresh tapers in the place of those that had burned out, and then he looked at his mother, revolving in his mind those apparently profound thoughts, those religious and philosophical commonplaces, which trouble people of mediocre minds in the face of death.

But he went downstairs as soon as his wife called him. She had written out a list of what had to be done during the morning, which rather frightened him when he saw it.

1. Lodge a declaration of death at the Town Hall.
2. See the coroner.
3. Order the coffin.
4. Give notice to the church.
5. Go to the undertaker.
6. Order the notices of her death at the printer's.
7. Go to the lawyer.
8. Telegraph the news to all the family.

Besides all this, there were a number of small commissions; so he took his hat and went out. As the news had got abroad, Madame Caravan's female friends and neighbours soon began to come in, and begged to be allowed to see the body. There had been a scene at the hairdresser's, on the ground floor, about the matter, between husband and wife, while he was shaving a customer. While busily knitting the woman had said: "Well, there is one less, and one as great a miser as one ever meets with. I certainly was not very fond of her; but, nevertheless, I must go and have a look at her."

The husband, while lathering his customer's chin, said:

"That is another queer fancy! Nobody but a woman would think of such a thing. It is not enough for them to worry you during life, but they cannot even leave you in peace when you are dead."

But his wife, not put out in the least, replied: "I can't help it; I must go. It has been on me since the morning. If I were not to see her, I should think about it all my life, but when I have had a good look at her, I shall be satisfied."

The knight of the razor shrugged his shoulders, and remarked in a low voice to the gentleman whose cheek he was scraping:

"Now, what sort of ideas do you think these confounded females have? I should not amuse myself by inspecting a corpse!"

But his wife heard him, and replied very quietly:

"But I do, I do." And then, putting her knitting down on the counter, she went upstairs, to the first floor, where she met two other neighbours. These had just come, and were discussing the event with Madame Caravan, who was giving them the details. Then the four went together to the mortuary chamber. The women went in softly, and, one after the other, sprinkled the bedclothes with the salted water, kneeled down, made the sign of the cross while they mumbled a prayer, then got up, and, open-mouthed, regarded the corpse for a long time, while the daughter-in-law of the dead woman, with her handkerchief to her face, pretended to be sobbing piteously.

When she turned to walk away, whom should she perceive standing close to the door but Marie-Louise and Philippe-Auguste, who were curiously taking stock of things. Then, forgetting to control her temper, she threw herself upon them with uplifted hand, crying out in a furious voice: "Will you get out of this, you brats."

Ten minutes later, going upstairs again with another contingent of neighbours, she prayed, wept profusely, performed all her duties, and again caught the children following her upstairs. She boxed their ears soundly, but the next time she paid no heed to them, and at each fresh influx of visitors the two urchins followed in the wake, crowded themselves up in a corner, slavishly imitating everything they saw their mother do.

When afternoon came round the crowds of curious people began to diminish, and soon there were no more visitors. Madame Caravan, returning to her own apartments, began to make the necessary preparations for the funeral ceremony, and the deceased was left by herself.

The window of the room was open. A torrid heat entered along with clouds of dust; the flames of the four candles were flickering in the direction of the corpse, and upon the cloth which covered the face, the closed eyes, the two hands stretched out, small flies alighted, came, went, and buzzed up and down incessantly, being the only companions of the old woman during the next hour.

Marie-Louise and Philippe-Auguste, however, had now left the house, and were running up and down the street. They were soon surrounded by their playmates, and by little girls, especially, who were older, and who were interested in the mysteries of life, and asked questions in the manner of persons of great importance.

"Then your grandmother is dead?"

"Yes, she died yesterday evening."

"What does a dead person look like?"

Then Marie began to explain, telling all about the candles, the sprig of box and the cadaverous face. It was not long before great curiosity was aroused in the breasts of all the children, and they asked to be allowed to go upstairs to look at the departed.

Then Marie-Louise arranged a party for the first visit, consisting of five girls and two boys — the biggest and the most courageous. She made them take off their shoes so that they might not be discovered. The troop filed into the house and mounted the stairs as stealthily as an army of mice.

Once in the chamber, the little girl, imitating her mother, regulated the ceremony. She solemnly walked in advance of her comrades, went down on her knees, made the sign of the cross, moistened the lips of the corpse with a few drops of water, stood up again, sprinkled the bed, and while the children all crowded together were approaching — frightened and curious, and eager to look at the face and hands of the deceased — she began suddenly to simulate sobbing, and to bury her eyes in her little handkerchief. Then, instantly consoled on thinking of the other children downstairs waiting at the door, she withdrew in haste, returning in a minute with another group, and then a third; for all the little ruffians of the neighbourhood, even to the little beggars in rags, had congregated in order to participate in this new pleasure. Each time she repeated her mother's grimaces with absolute perfection.

At length, however, she tired of it. Some game

or another attracted the children away from the house, and the old grandmother was left alone, forgotten suddenly by everybody.

A dismal gloom pervaded the chamber, and upon the dry and rigid features of the corpse the dying flames of the candles cast occasional gleams of light.

Toward eight o'clock, Caravan ascended to the chamber of death, closed the windows, and renewed the candles. On entering now he was quite composed, evidently accustomed to regard the corpse as though it had been there for a month. He even went the length of declaring that, as yet, there were no signs of decomposition, making this remark just at the moment when he and his wife were about to sit down at table. "Pshaw!" she responded, "she is made of wood; she will keep for a year."

The soup was eaten without a word being uttered by anyone. The children, who had been free all day, were now worn out by fatigue and were sleeping soundly in their chairs, and nobody ventured to break the silence.

Suddenly the flame of the lamp went down. Madame Caravan immediately turned up the wick, a prolonged, gurgling noise ensued, and the light went out. She had forgotten to buy oil during the day. To send for it now to the grocer's would keep back the dinner, and everybody began to look for candles. But none were to be found except the night lights which had been placed upon the table upstairs, in the death-chamber.

Madame Caravan, always prompt in her decisions, quickly dispatched Marie-Louise to fetch two, and her return was awaited in total darkness.

The footsteps of the girl who had ascended the stairs were distinctly heard. Then followed silence for a few seconds, and then the child descended precipitately. She threw open the door affrighted, and in a choked voice murmured: "Oh! papa, grandmamma is dressing herself!"

Caravan bounded to his feet with such precipitation that his chair rolled over against another chair. He stammered out: "What! What do you say?"

But Marie-Louise, gasping with emotion, repeated: "Grand — grand — grandmamma is putting on her clothes, and is coming downstairs."

Caravan rushed boldly up the staircase, followed by his wife, dumbfounded; but he came to a standstill before the door of the room, overcome with terror, not daring to enter. What was he going to see? Madame Caravan, more courageous, turned the handle of the door and stepped forward into the room.

The room seemed to be darker, and in the middle of it, a tall emaciated figure moved about. The old woman stood upright, and in awakening from her lethargic sleep, before even full consciousness had returned to her, in turning upon her side and raising herself on her elbow, she had extinguished three of the candles which burned near the mortuary bed. Then, recovering her strength, she got out of bed and began to look for her things. The absence of her chest of drawers had at first given her some trouble, but, after a little, she had succeeded in finding her things at the bottom of the wooden trunk, and was now quietly dressing. She emptied the dishful of salted water, replaced the box which contained the latter behind the looking-glass, arranged the chairs in their places, and was ready to go downstairs when her son and daughter-in-law appeared.

Caravan rushed forward, seized her by the hands, and embraced her with tears in his eyes, while his wife, who was behind him, repeated in a hypocritical tone of voice: "Oh, what a blessing! Oh, what a blessing!"

But the old woman, not at all moved, without even appearing to understand, as rigid as a statue, and with glazed eyes, simply asked: "Will dinner soon be ready?"

He stammered out, not knowing what he said:

"Oh, yes, mother, we have been waiting for you."

And with an alacrity unusual in him he took her arm, while Madame Caravan the younger seized the candle and lighted them downstairs, walking backward in front of them, step by step, just as she had done the previous night, in front of her husband, when he was carrying the marble.

On reaching the first floor, she ran against people who were ascending. It was the family from Charenton, Madame Braux, followed by her husband.

The wife, tall and fleshy, with the stomach of a victim of dropsy, opened wide her astonished eyes, ready to take flight. The husband, a shoemaker and socialist, a little hairy man, the perfect image of a monkey, murmured, quite unconcerned: "Well, what next? Is she resurrected?"

As soon as Madame Caravan recognized them, she made despairing signs to them; then speaking aloud, she said: "Mercy! How do you mean! Look there! What a happy surprise!"

But Madame Braux, dumbfounded, understood nothing. She responded in a low voice: "It was your telegram which made us come; we believed it was all over."

Her husband, who was behind her, pinched her to make her keep silent. He added with a malignant laugh, which his thick beard concealed: "It was very kind of you to invite us here. We set out in post-haste" — a remark which showed clearly the hostility that for a long time had reigned between the households. Then, just as the old woman had arrived at the last steps, he pushed forward quickly and rubbed against her cheeks the hair which covered his face, bawling out in her ear, on account of her deafness: "How well you look, mother; sturdy as usual, hey!"

Madame Braux, in her amazement at seeing the old woman alive whom they all believed to be dead, dared not even embrace her; and her enormous bulk blocked up the passage and hindered the others from advancing. The old woman, uneasy and suspicious, but without speaking, looked at everyone around her. Her little gray eyes, piercing and hard, fixed themselves now on the one and now on the other, full of thoughts which could be read by her embarrassed children.

Caravan, to explain matters, said: "She has

been somewhat ill, but she is better now — quite well, indeed, are you not, mother?"

Then the good woman, stopping in her walk, responded in a husky voice, as though it came from a distance: "It was catalepsy. I heard you all the while."

An embarrassing silence followed. They entered the dining-room, and in a few minutes sat down to an improvised dinner.

Only Monsieur Braux had retained his self-possession; his gorilla features grinned wickedly, while he let fall some words of double meaning which painfully disconcerted everyone.

But the bell in the hall kept on ringing every second; and Rosalie, who had lost her head, came looking for Caravan, who dashed out, throwing down his napkin. His brother-in-law even asked him whether it was not one of his visiting days, to which he stammered out, "No, a few messages; nothing of importance."

Next, a packet was brought in, which he began to open without thinking, and the death announcements, with black borders, appeared. Reddening up to the very eyes, Caravan closed the envelope, and pushed it into his waistcoat pocket.

His mother had not seen it! She was looking intently at her clock, which stood on the mantelpiece, and the embarrassment increased in midst of a glacial silence. Turning her wrinked old witch's face toward her daughter, the old woman, from whose eyes flashed fierce malice, said:

"On Monday bring me your little girl. I want so much to see her."

Madame Braux, her features illuminated, exclaimed: "Yes, mother, I will," while Madame Caravan, the younger, became pale, and seemed to be enduring the most excruciating agony. The two men, however, gradually drifted into conversation, and soon became embroiled in a political discussion. Braux maintained the most revolutionary and communistic doctrines, gesticulating and throwing about his arms, his eyes gleaming in his hairy countenance.

"Property, sir," he said, "is a robbery perpetrated on the working classes; the land is the common property of every man; hereditary rights are an infamy and a disgrace." But, hereupon, he suddenly stopped, having all the appearance of a man who has just said something foolish: then, resuming, after a pause, he said in softer tones: "But, I can see quite well that this is not the proper moment to discuss things."

The door was opened, and "Doctor" Chenet appeared. For a moment he seemed bewildered, but regaining his composure, he approached the old woman, and said:

"Ah, ha! mamma, you are better to-day. Oh! I never had any doubt but you would come round again; in fact, I said to myself as I was mounting the staircase: 'I have an idea that I shall find the old woman on her feet once more.'" Then he tapped her gently on the back: "Ah! she is as solid as the Pont-Neuf, she will bury us all out: you will see if she does not."

He sat down, accepted the coffee that was offered him. and soon began to join in the conversation of the two men, backing up Braux, for he himself had been mixed up in the Commune.

Now the old woman, feeling herself fatigued, wished to leave the room, at which Caravan rushed forward. She thereupon looked him in the eyes and said to him:

"You must carry my clock and chest of drawers upstairs again without a moment's delay."

"Yes, mamma," he replied, stammering; "yes, I will do so."

The old woman then took the arm of her daughter and withdrew from the room. The two Caravans remained rooted to the floor, silent, plunged in the deepest despair, while Braux rubbed his hands and sipped his coffee, gleefully.

Suddenly Madame Caravan, consumed with rage, attacked him, exclaiming: "You are a thief, a scoundrel, a cur. I would spit in your face, if — I would — I — would —" She could find nothing further to say, suffocating as she was with rage, while Braux still sipped his coffee, laughing.

His wife, returning just then, rushed at her sister-in-law, and both — the one with her enormous bulk, the other, epileptic and spare — with angry voices and hands trembling, hurled wild insults at each other.

Chenet and Braux now interposed, and the latter, taking his better half by the shoulders, pushed her out of the door in front of him, shouting:

"Get out, you ass: you make too much noise." Then the two were heard in the street quarrelling with each other, until they had disappeared in the distance.

Monsieur Chenet also took his departure, leaving the Caravans alone, face to face. The husband fell back in his chair, and with the cold sweat standing out in beads on his temples murmured: "What on earth shall I say at the office?"

ON THE RIVER

LAST summer I rented a country cottage on the banks of the Seine, several miles from Paris, and I used to go out to sleep there every night. After a while, I formed the acquaintance of one of my neighbours, a man between thirty and forty years of age, who really was one of the queerest characters I have ever met. He was an old boating-man, crazy on the subject of boats, and was always either in, or on, or by the water. He must have been born in a boat, and probably he will die in one, some day, while taking a last outing.

One evening, as we were walking along the banks of the Seine, I asked him to tell me about some of his nautical experiences. Immediately his face lighted up, and he became eloquent, almost poetical, for his heart was full of an all-absorbing, irresistible, devouring passion — a love for the river.

"Ah!" said he, "how many recollections I have of the river that flows at our feet! You street-dwellers have no idea what the river really is. But let a fisherman pronounce the word. To him it means mystery, the unknown, a land of mirage and phantasmagoria, where odd things that have no real existence are seen at night and strange noises are heard; where one trembles without knowing the reason why, as when passing through a cemetery, — and indeed the river is a sinister cemetery without graves.

"Land, for a fisherman, has boundaries, but the river, on moonless nights, appears to him unlimited A sailor doesn't feel the same way about the sea. The sea is often cruel, but it roars and foams, it gives us fair warning; the river is silent and treacherous. It flows stealthily, without a murmur, and the eternal gentle motion of the water is more awful to me than the big ocean waves.

"Dreamers believe that the deep hides immense lands of blue, where the drowned roll around among the big fish, in strange forests or in crystal caves. The river has only black depths, where the dead decay in the slime. But it's beautiful when the sun shines on it, and the waters splash softly on the banks covered with whispering reeds.

"In speaking of the ocean the poet says:

"'O flots, que vous savez de lugubres histoires!
Flots profonds, redoutés des mères à genoux,
Vous vous les racontez en montant les marées,
Et c'est ce qui vous fait ces voix désespérées
Que vous avez, le soir, quand vous venez vers nous.'

Well, I believe that the stories the slender reeds tell one another in their wee, silvery voices are even more appalling than the ghastly tragedies related by the roaring waves.

"But as you have asked me to relate some of my recollections, I will tell you a strange adventure that happened to me here, about ten years ago.

"Then, as now, I lived in old mother Lafon's house and one of my best friends, Louis Bernet, who since has given up boating, as well as his happy-go-lucky ways, to become a State Councillor, was camping out in the village of C——, two miles away. We used to take dinner together every day, either at his place or at mine.

"One evening, as I was returning home alone, feeling rather tired, and with difficulty rowing the twelve-foot boat that I always took out at night, I stopped to rest a little while near that point over there, formed by reeds, about two hundred yards in front of the railway bridge. The weather was magnificent; the moon was shining very brightly, and the air was soft and still. The calmness of the surroundings tempted me, and I thought how pleasant it would be to fill my pipe here and smoke. No sooner said than done, and, laying hold of the anchor, I dropped it overboard. The boat, which was following the stream, slid to the end of the chain and came to a stop; I settled myself aft on a rug, as comfortably as I could. There was not a sound to be heard nor a movement to be seen, though sometimes I noticed the almost imperceptible rippling of the water on the banks, and watched the highest clumps of reeds, which at times assumed strange shapes that appeared to move.

"The river was perfectly calm, but I was affected by the extraordinary stillness that enveloped me. The frogs and toads, the nocturnal musicians of the swamps, were voiceless. Suddenly, at my right, a frog croaked. I started; it stopped, and all was silent. I resolved to light my pipe for distraction. But, strange to say, though I was an inveterate smoker I failed to enjoy it, and after a few puffs

I grew sick and stopped smoking. Then I began to hum an air, but the sound of my voice depressed me.

"At last I lay down in the boat and watched the sky. For a while I remained quiet, but presently the slight pitching of the boat disturbed me. I felt as if it were swaying to and fro from one side of the river to the other, and that an invisible force or being was drawing it slowly to the bottom and then raising it to let it drop again. I was knocked about as if in a storm; I heard strange noises; I jumped up; the water was shining and all was still. Then I knew that my nerves were slightly shaken, and decided to leave the river. I pulled on the chain. The boat moved along, but presently I felt some resistance and pulled harder. The anchor refused to come up; it had caught in something at the bottom and remained stuck. I pulled and tugged but to no avail. With the oars I turned the boat around and forced her up-stream, in order to alter the position of the anchor. This was all in vain, however, for the anchor did not yield; so in a rage, I began to shake at the chain, which wouldn't budge.

"I sat down discouraged, to ponder over my mishap. It was impossible to break the chain or to separate it from the boat, as it was enormous and was riveted to a piece of wood as big as my arm; but as the weather continued fine, I did not doubt but that some fisherman would come along and rescue me. The accident calmed me so much that I managed to remain quiet and smoke my pipe. I had a bottle of rum with me so I drank two or three glasses of it and began to laugh at my situation. It was so warm that it would not have mattered much had I been obliged to spend all night out of doors.

"Suddenly something jarred slightly against the side of the boat. I started, and a cold sweat broke over me from head to foot. The noise was due to a piece of wood drifting along with the current, but it proved sufficient to disturb my mind, and once more I seized the chain and tugged in desperation. I felt the same strange nervousness creep over me. The anchor remained firm. I seated myself again, exhausted.

"Meantime the river was covering itself with a white mist that lay close to the water, so that when I stood up neither the stream, nor my feet, nor the boat, were visible to me; I could distinguish only the ends of the reeds and, a little farther away, the meadow, ashen in the moonlight, with large black patches formed by groups of Italian poplars reaching toward the sky. I was buried up to my waist in something that looked like a blanket of down of a peculiar whiteness; and all kinds of fantastic visions arose before me. I imagined that some one was trying to crawl into the boat, which I could no longer see, and that the river hidden under the thick fog was full of strange creatures that were swimming all around me. I felt a horrible depression steal over me, my temples throbbed, my heart beat wildly, and, losing all control over myself, I was ready to plunge overboard and swim to safety. But this idea suddenly filled me with horror. I imagined myself lost in the dense mist, floundering about aimlessly among the reeds and water-plants, unable to find the banks of the river or the boat; and I felt as if I should certainly be drawn by my feet to the bottom of the dark waters. As I really should have had to swim against the current for at least five hundred yards before reaching a spot where I could safely land, it was nine chances to ten that, being unable to see in the fog, I should drown, although I was a fine swimmer.

"I tried to overcome my dread. I determined not to be afraid, but there was something in me besides my will and that something was faint-hearted. I asked myself what there was to fear; my courageous self railed at the other, the timid one; never before had I so fully realised the opposition that exists between the two beings we have in us; the one willing, the other resisting, and each one triumphing in turn. But this foolish and unaccountable fear was growing worse and worse, and was becoming positive terror. I remained motionless, with open eyes and straining ears, waiting. For what? I scarcely knew, but it must have been for something terrible. I believe that had a fish suddenly taken it into its head to jump out of the water, as frequently happens, I should have fallen in a dead faint. However, I managed to keep my senses after a violent effort to control myself. I took my bottle of rum and again raised it to my lips.

"Suddenly I began to shout at the top of my voice, turning successively toward the four points of the horizon. After my throat had become comletely paralysed with shouting, I listened. A dog was barking in the distance.

"I drank some more rum and lay down in the bottom of the boat. I remained thus at least one hour, perhaps two, without sleeping, my eyes open, visited by nightmares. I did not dare to sit up, though I had an insane desire to do so; I put it off from second to second, saying: 'Now then, I'll get up,' but I was afraid to move. At last I raised myself with infinite care, as if my life depended on the slightest sound I might make, and peered over the edge of the boat. I was greeted by the most marvellous, stupendous sight that it is possible to imagine. It was a vision of fairyland, one of those phenomena that travellers in distant countries tell us about, but that we are unable to believe.

"The mist, which two hours ago hung over the water, had lifted and settled on the banks of the stream. It formed on each side an unbroken hill, six or seven yards in height, that shone in the moonlight with the dazzling whiteness of snow. Nothing could be seen but the flashing river, moving between the two white mountains, and overhead a full moon that illuminated the milky-blue sky.

"All the hosts of the water had awakened; the frogs were croaking dismally, while from time to time a toad sent its short, monotonous, and gloomy note to the stars. Strange to say, I was no longer frightened; I was surrounded by a landscape so utterly unreal that the strangest freaks of nature would not have surprised me at all.

"How long this situation lasted I am unable to tell, for I finally dozed off to sleep. When I awoke, the moon was gone and the sky was covered with clouds. The water splashed dismally, the wind was blowing, it was cold and completely dark. I finished the rum and lay listening to the rustling of the reeds and the murmur of the river. I tried to see, but failed to distinguish the boat or even my hands, although I held them close to my eyes. The darkness, however, was slowly decreasing. Suddenly I thought I saw a shadow glide past me. I shouted to it and a voice responded: it was a fisherman. I called to him and told him of my plight. He brought his boat alongside mine and both began tugging at the chain. The anchor still would not yield. A cold, rainy day was setting in, one of those days that bring disaster and sadness. I perceived another boat, which we hailed. The owner added his strength to ours, and little by little the anchor gave way. It came up very slowly, laden with considerable weight. Finally a black heap appeared and we dragged it into my boat. It was the body of an old woman, with a big stone tied around her neck!"

PAUL'S MISTRESS

THE Restaurant Grillon, a small commonwealth of boatmen, was slowly emptying. In front of the door all was tumult — cries and calls — and huge fellows in white jerseys gesticulated with oars on their shoulders.

The ladies in bright spring toilettes stepped aboard the skiffs with care, and seating themselves astern, arranged their dresses, while the landlord of the establishment, a mighty, red-bearded, self-possessed individual of renowned strength, offered his hand to the pretty creatures, and kept the frail crafts steady.

The rowers, bare-armed, with bulging chests, took their places in their turn, playing to the gallery as they did so — a gallery consisting of middle-class people dressed in their Sunday clothes, of workmen and soldiers leaning upon their elbows on the parapet of the bridge, all taking a great interest in the sight.

One by one the boats cast off from the landing stage. The oarsmen bent forward and then threw themselves backward with even swing, and under the impetus of the long curved oars, the swift skiffs glided along the river, grew smaller in the distance, and finally disappeared under the railway bridge, as they descended the stream toward La Grenouillère. One couple only remained behind. The young man, still almost beardless, slender, with a pale countenance, held his mistress, a thin little brunette with the air of a grasshopper, by the waist; and occasionally they gazed into each other's eyes. The landlord shouted:

"Come, Mr. Paul, make haste," and they drew near.

Of all the guests of the house, Mr. Paul was the most liked and most respected. He paid well and punctually, while the others hung back for a long time if indeed they did not vanish without paying. Besides which he was a sort of walking advertisement for the establishment, inasmuch as his father was a senator. When a stranger would inquire: "Who on earth is that little chap who thinks so much of his girl?" some *habitué* would reply, half-aloud, with a mysterious and important air: "Don't you know? That is Paul Baron, a senator's son."

And invariably the other would exclaim:

"Poor devil! He has got it badly."

Mother Grillon, a good and worthy business woman, described the young man and his companion as "her two turtledoves," and appeared quite touched by this passion, which was profitable for her business.

The couple advanced at a slow pace. The skiff "Madeleine" was ready, and at the moment of embarking they kissed each other, which caused the public collected on the bridge to laugh. Mr. Paul took the oars, and rowed away for La Grenouillère.

When they arrived it was just upon three o'clock and the large floating café overflowed with people.

The immense raft, sheltered by a tarpaulin roof, is joined to the charming island of Croissy by two narrow footbridges, one of which leads into the centre of the aquatic establishment, while the other unites with a tiny islet, planted with a tree and called "The Flower Pot," and thence leads to land near the bath office.

Mr. Paul made fast his boat alongside the establishment, climbed over the railing of the café, and then, grasping his mistress's hands, assisted her out of the boat. They both seated themselves at the end of a table opposite each other.

On the opposite side of the river along the towing-path, a long string of vehicles was drawn up. Cabs alternated with the fine carriages of the swells; the first, clumsy, with enormous bodies crushing the springs, drawn by broken-down hacks with hanging heads and broken knees; the second, slightly built on light wheels, with horses slender and straight, their heads well up, their bits snowy with foam, and with solemn coachmen in livery, heads erect in high collars, waiting bolt upright, with whips resting on their knees.

The bank was covered with people who came off in families, or in parties, or in couples, or alone. They plucked at the blades of grass, went down to the water, ascended the path, and having reached the spot, stood still awaiting the ferryman. The clumsy punt plied incessantly from bank to bank, discharging its passengers upon the island. The arm of the river (called the Dead Arm) upon which this refreshment wharf lay, seemed asleep, so feeble was the current. Fleets of yawls, of skiffs, of canoes, of podoscaphs, of gigs, of craft of all forms and of all kinds, crept about upon the motionless stream, crossing each other, intermingling, running foul of one another, stopping abruptly under a jerk of the arms only to shoot off afresh under a sudden strain of the muscles and gliding swiftly along like great yellow or red fishes.

Others arrived continually; some from Chatou up the stream; others from Bougival down it; laughter crossed the water from one boat to another, calls, admonitions, or imprecations. The boatmen exposed the bronzed and knotted muscles of their biceps to the heat of the day; and like strange floating flowers, the silk parasols, red, green, blue, or yellow, of the ladies bloomed in the sterns of the boats.

A July sun flamed high in the heavens; the atmosphere seemed full of burning merriment; not a breath of air stirred the leaves of the willows or poplars.

In front, away in the distance, the inevitable Mont-Valérien reared its fortified ramparts, tier above tier, in the intense light; while on the right the divine slopes of Louveciennes, following the bend of the river, disposed themselves in a semicircle, displaying in turn across the rich and shady lawns of large gardens the white walls of country seats.

Upon the outskirts of La Grenouillère a crowd of pedestrians moved about beneath the giant trees which make this corner of the island one of the most delightful parks in the world.

Women and girls with yellow hair and breasts developed beyond all measurement, with exaggerated hips, their complexions plastered with rouge, their eyes daubed with charcoal, their lips blood-red, laced up, rigged out in outrageous dresses, trailed the crying bad taste of their toilettes over the fresh green sward; while beside them young men posed in their fashion-plate garments with light gloves, patent leather boots, canes the size of a thread, and single eyeglasses emphasizing the insipidity of their smiles.

Opposite La Grenouillère the island is narrow, and on its other side, where also a ferryboat plies, bringing people unceasingly across from Croissy, the rapid branch of the river, full of whirlpools and eddies and foam, rushes along with the strength of a torrent. A detachment of pontoon-builders, in the uniform of artillerymen, was encamped upon this bank, and the soldiers seated in a row on a long beam watched the water flowing.

In the floating establishment there was a boisterous and uproarious crowd. The wooden tables upon which the spilt refreshments made little sticky streams were covered with half-empty glasses and surrounded by half-tipsy individuals. The crowd shouted, sang, and brawled. The men, their hats at the backs of their heads, their faces red, with the shining eyes of drunkards, moved about vociferating and evidently looking for the quarrels natural to brutes. The women, seeking their prey for the night, sought for free liquor in the meantime; and the unoccupied space between the tables was dominated by the customary local public, a whole regiment of rowdy boatmen, with their female companions in short flannel skirts

One of them performed on the piano and appeared to play with his feet as well as his hands; four couples glided through a quadrille, and some young men watched them, polished and correct, men who would have looked respectable, did not their innate viciousness show in spite of everything.

For there you see all the scum of society, all its well-bred debauchery, all the seamy side of Parisian society — a mixture of counter-jumpers, of strolling players, of low journalists, of gentlemen in tutelage, of rotten stock-jobbers, of ill-famed debauchees, of old used-up fast men; a doubtful crowd of suspicious characters, half-known, half-sunk, half-recognised, half-criminal, pickpockets, rogues, procurers of women, sharpers with dignified manners, and a bragging air which seems to say: "I shall kill the first man who treats me as a scoundrel."

The place reeks of folly, and stinks of vulgarity and cheap gallantry. Male and female are just as bad one as the other. There dwells an odour of so-called love, and there one fights for a yes, or for a no, in order to sustain a worm-eaten reputation, which a thrust of the sword or a pistol bullet only destroys further.

Some of the neighbouring inhabitants looked in out of curiosity every Sunday; some young men, very young, appeared there every year to learn how to live, some promenaders lounging about showed themselves there; some greenhorns wandered thither. With good reason is it named La Grenouillère. At the side of the covered wharf where drink was served, and quite close to the Flower Pot, people bathed. Those among the women who possessed the requisite roundness of form came there to display their wares and to get clients. The rest, scornful, although well filled out with wadding, supported by springs, corrected here and altered there, watched their dabbling sisters with disdain.

The swimmers crowded on to a little platform to dive. Straight like vine poles, or round like pumpkins, gnarled like olive branches, bowed over in front, or thrown backward by the size of their stomachs, and invariably ugly, they leaped into the water, splashing it over the drinkers in the café.

Notwithstanding the great trees which overhang the floating-house, and notwithstanding the vicinity of the water, a suffocating heat filled the place. The fumes of the spilt liquors mingled with the effluvia of the bodies and with the strong perfumes with which the skin of the trader in love is saturated and which evaporate in this furnace. But beneath all these diverse scents a slight aroma of *poudre de riz* lingered, disappearing and reappearing, and perpetually encountered as though some concealed hand had shaken an invisible powder-puff in the air. The show was on the river, where the perpetual coming and going of the boats attracted the eyes. The girls in the boats sprawled upon their seats opposite their strong-wristed males, and scornfully contemplated the dinner-hunting females prowling about the island.

Sometimes when a crew in full swing passed at top speed, the friends who had gone ashore gave vent to shouts, and all the people as if suddenly seized with madness commenced to yell.

At the bend of the river toward Chatou fresh boats continually appeared. They came nearer and grew larger, and as faces became recognisable, the vociferations broke out anew.

A canoe covered with an awning and manned by four women came slowly down the current. She who rowed was petite, thin, faded, in a cabin-boy's costume, her hair drawn up under an oilskin hat. Opposite her, a lusty blonde, dressed as a man, with a white flannel jacket, lay upon her back at the bottom of the boat, her legs in the air, resting on the seat at each side of the rower. She smoked a cigarette, while at each stroke of the oars, her chest and her stomach quivered, shaken by the stroke. At the back, under the awning, two handsome girls, tall and slender, one dark and the other fair, held each other by the waist as they watched their companions.

A cry arose from La Grenouillère, "There's Lesbos," and all at once a furious clamour, a terrifying scramble took place; the glasses were knocked down; people clambered on to the tables; all in a frenzy of noise bawled: "Lesbos! Lesbos! Lesbos!" The shout rolled along, became indistinct, was no longer more than a kind of deafening howl, and then suddenly it seemed to start anew, to rise into space, to cover the plain, to fill the foliage of the great trees, to extend to the distant slopes, and reach even to the sun.

The rower, in the face of this ovation, had quietly stopped. The handsome blonde, stretched out upon the bottom of the boat, turned her head with a careless air, as she raised herself upon her elbows;

and the two girls at the back commenced laughing as they saluted the crowd.

Then the hullabaloo redoubled, making the floating establishment tremble. The men took off their hats, the women waved their handkerchiefs, and all voices, shrill or deep, together cried:

"Lesbos."

It was as if these people, this collection of the corrupt, saluted their chiefs like the war-ships which fire guns when an admiral passes along the line.

The numerous fleet of boats also saluted the women's boat, which pushed along more quickly to land farther off.

Mr. Paul, contrary to the others, had drawn a key from his pocket and whistled with all his might. His nervous mistress grew paler, caught him by the arm to make him be quiet, and upon this occasion she looked at him with fury in her eyes. But he appeared exasperated, as though borne away by jealousy of some man or by deep anger, instinctive and ungovernable. He stammered, his lips quivering with indignation:

"It is shameful! They ought to be drowned like puppies with a stone about the neck."

But Madeleine instantly flew into a rage; her small and shrill voice became a hiss, and she spoke volubly, as though pleading her own cause:

"And what has it to do with you — you indeed? Are they not at liberty to do what they wish since they owe nobody anything? You shut up and mind your own business."

But he cut her speech short:

"It is the police whom it concerns, and I will have them marched off to St. Lazare; indeed I will."

She gave a start:

"You?"

"Yes, I! And in the meantime I forbid you to speak to them — you understand, I forbid you to do so."

Then she shrugged her shoulders and grew calm in a moment:

"My dear, I shall do as I please; if you are not satisfied, be off, and instantly. I am not your wife, am I? Very well then, hold your tongue."

He made no reply and they stood face to face, their lips tightly closed, breathing quickly.

At the other end of the great wooden café the four women made their entry. The two in men's costumes marched in front: the one thin like an oldish tomboy, with a yellow tinge on her temples; the other filling out her white flannel garments with her fat, swelling out her wide trousers with her buttocks and swaying about like a fat goose with enormous legs and yielding knees. Their two friends followed them, and the crowd of boatmen thronged about to shake their hands.

The four had hired a small cottage close to the water's edge, and lived there as two households would have lived.

Their vice was public, recognised, patent to all. People talked of it as a natural thing, which almost excited their sympathy, and whispered in very low tones strange stories of dramas begotten of furious feminine jealousies, of the stealthy visit of well-known women and of actresses to the little house close to the water's edge.

A neighbour, horrified by these scandalous rumours, notified the police, and the inspector, accompanied by a man, had come to make inquiry. The mission was a delicate one; it was impossible, in short, to accuse these women, who did not abandon themselves to prostitution, of any tangible crime. The inspector, very much puzzled, and, indeed, ignorant of the nature of the offences suspected, had asked questions at random, and made a lofty report conclusive of their innocence.

The joke spread as far as Saint Germain. They walked about the Grenouillère establishment with mincing steps like queens; and seemed to glory in their fame, rejoicing in the gaze that was fixed on them, so superior to this crowd, to this mob, to these plebeians.

Madeleine and her lover watched them approach, and the girl's eyes lit up.

When the first two had reached the end of the table, Madeleine cried:

"Pauline!"

The large woman turned and stopped, continuing all the time to hold the arm of her feminine cabin-boy:

"Good gracious, Madeleine! Do come and talk to me, my dear."

Paul squeezed his fingers upon his mistress's wrist, but she said to him, with such an air: "You know, my dear, you can clear out, if you like," that he said nothing and remained alone.

Then they chatted in low voices, all three of them standing. Many pleasant jests passed their lips, they spoke quickly; and Pauline now and then looked at Paul, by stealth, with a shrewd and malicious smile.

At last, unable to put up with it any longer, he suddenly rose and in a single bound was at their side, trembling in every limb. He seized Madeleine by the shoulders.

"Come, I wish it," said he; "I have forbidden you to speak to these sluts."

Whereupon Pauline raised her voice and set to work blackguarding him with her Billingsgate vocabulary. All the bystanders laughed; they drew near him; they raised themselves on tiptoe in order the better to see him. He remained dumb under this downpour of filthy abuse. It appeared to him that the words which came from that mouth and fell upon him defiled him like dirt, and, in presence of the row which was beginning, he fell back, retraced his steps, and rested his elbows on the railing toward the river, turning his back upon the victorious women.

There he stayed watching the water, and sometimes with rapid gesture, as though he could pluck it out, he removed with his nervous fingers the tear which stood in his eye.

The fact was that he was hopelessly in love, without knowing why, notwithstanding his refined instincts, in spite of his reason, in spite, indeed, of his will. He had fallen into this love as one falls into a muddy hole. Of a tender and delicate disposition, he had dreamed of liaisons, exquisite, ideal, and impassioned, and there that little bit of a woman, stupid like all prostitutes, with an exasperating stupidity, not even pretty, but thin and a spitfire, had taken him prisoner, possessing him from head to foot, body and soul. He had submitted to this feminine witchery, mysterious and all powerful, this unknown power, this prodigious domination — arising no one knows whence, but from the demon of the flesh — which casts the most sensible man at the feet of some harlot or other without there being anything in her to explain her fatal and sovereign power.

And there at his back he felt that some infamous thing was brewing. Shouts of laughter cut him to the heart. What should he do? He knew well, but he could not do it.

He steadily watched an angler upon the bank opposite him, and his motionless line.

Suddenly, the worthy man jerked a little silver fish, which wriggled at the end of his line, out of the river. Then he endeavoured to extract his hook, pulled and turned it, but in vain. At last, losing patience, he commenced to tear it out, and all the bleeding gullet of the fish, with a portion of its intestines came out. Paul shuddered, rent to his heartstrings. It seemed to him that the hook was his love, and that if he should pluck it out, all that he had in his breast would come out in the same way at the end of a curved iron, fixed in the depths of his being, to which Madeleine held the line.

A hand was placed upon his shoulder; he started and turned; his mistress was at his side. They did not speak to each other; and like him she rested her elbows upon the railing, and fixed her eyes upon the river.

He tried to speak to her and could find nothing. He could not even disentangle his own emotions; all that he was sensible of was joy at feeling her there close to him, come back again, as well as shameful cowardice, a craving to pardon everything, to allow everything, provided she never left him.

At last, after a few minutes, he asked her in a very gentle voice:

"Would you like to go? It will be nicer in the boat."

She answered: "Yes, darling."

And he assisted her into the skiff, pressing her hands, all softened, with some tears still in his eyes. Then she looked at him with a smile and they kissed each other again.

They reascended the river very slowly, skirting the willow-bordered, grass-covered bank, bathed and still in the afternoon warmth. When they had returned to the Restaurant Grillon, it was barely six o'clock. Then leaving their boat they set off on foot towards Bezons, across the fields and along the high poplars which bordered the river. The long grass ready to be mowed was full of flowers. The sinking sun glowed from beneath a sheet of red light, and in the tempered heat of the closing day the floating exhalations from the grass, mingled with the damp scents from the river, filled the air with a soft languor, with a happy light, with an atmosphere of blessing.

A soft weakness overtook his heart, a species of communion with this splendid calm of evening, with this vague and mysterious throb of teeming life, with the keen and melancholy poetry which seems to arise from flowers and things, and reveals itself to the senses at this sweet and pensive time.

Paul felt all that; but for her part she did not understand anything of it. They walked side by side; and, suddenly, tired of being silent, she sang. She sang in her shrill, unmusical voice some street song, some catchy air, which jarred upon the profound and serene harmony of the evening.

Then he looked at her and felt an impassable abyss between them. She beat the grass with her parasol, her head slightly inclined, admiring her feet and singing, dwelling on the notes, attempting trills, and venturing on shakes. Her smooth little brow, of which he was so fond, was at that time absolutely empty! empty! There was nothing therein but this canary music; and the ideas which formed there by chance were like this music. She did not understand anything of him; they were now as separated as if they did not live together. Did his kisses never go any farther than her lips?

Then she raised her eyes to him and laughed again. He was moved to the quick and, extending his arms in a paroxysm of love, he embraced her passionately.

As he was rumpling her dress she finally broke away from him, murmuring by way of compensation as she did so:

"That's enough. You know I love you, my darling."

But he clasped her around the waist and, seized by madness, he started to run with her. He kissed her on the cheek, on the temple, on the neck, all the while dancing with joy. They threw themselves down panting at the edge of a thicket, lit up by the rays of the setting sun, and before they had recovered breath they were in one another's arms without her understanding his transport.

They returned, holding each other by the hand, when, suddenly, through the trees, they perceived on the river the skiff manned by the four women. Fat Pauline also saw them, for she drew herself up and blew kisses to Madeleine. And then she cried:

"Until to-night!"

Madeleine replied: "Until to-night!"

Paul felt as if his heart had suddenly been frozen.

They re-entered the house for dinner and installed themselves in one of the arbours, close to the water. They began to eat in silence. When night arrived, the waiter brought a candle enclosed in a glass globe, which gave a feeble and glimmering light; and they heard every moment the bursts of shouting from the boatmen in the large room on the first floor.

Toward dessert, Paul, taking Madeleine's hand, tenderly said to her:

"I feel very tired, my darling; unless you have any objection, we will go to bed early."

She, however, understood the ruse, and shot an enigmatical glance at him — that glance of treachery which so readily appears in the depths of a woman's eyes. Having reflected she answered:

"You can go to bed if you wish, but I have promised to go to the ball at La Grenouillère."

He smiled in a piteous manner, one of those

smiles with which one veils the most horrible suffering, and replied in a coaxing but agonized tone:

"If you were really nice, we should remain here, both of us."

She indicated no with her head, without opening her mouth.

He insisted:

"I beg of you, my darling."

Then she roughly broke out:

"You know what I said to you. If you are not satisfied, the door is open. No one wishes to keep you. As for myself, I have promised; I shall go."

He placed his two elbows upon the table, covered his face with his hands, and remained there pondering sorrowfully.

The boat people came down again, shouting as usual, and set off in their vessels for the ball at La Grenouillère.

Madeleine said to Paul:

"If you are not coming, say so, and I will ask one of these gentlemen to take me."

Paul rose:

"Let us go!" murmured he.

And they left.

The night was black, the sky full of stars, but the air was heat-laden by oppressive breaths of wind, burdened with emanations, and with living germs, which destroyed the freshness of the night. It offered a heated caress, made one breathe more quickly, gasp a little, so thick and heavy did it seem. The boats started on their way, bearing Venetian lanterns at the prow. It was not possible to distinguish the craft, but only the little coloured lights, swift and dancing up and down like frenzied glowworms, while voices sounded from all sides in the shadows. The young people's skiff glided gently along. Now and then, when a fast boat passed near them, they could, for a moment, see the white back of the rower, lit up by his lantern.

When they turned the elbow of the river, La Grenouillère appeared to them in the distance. The establishment *en fête*, was decorated with flags and garlands of coloured lights, in grape-like clusters. On the Seine some great barges moved about slowly, representing domes, pyramids, and elaborate monuments in fires of all colours. Illuminated festoons hung right down to the water, and sometimes a red or blue lantern, at the end of an immense invisible fishing-rod, seemed like a great swinging star.

All this illumination spread a light around the café, lit up the great trees on the bank, from top to bottom, the trunks standing out in pale gray and the leaves in milky green upon the deep black of the fields and the heavens. The orchestra, composed of five suburban artists, flung far its public-house dance-music, poor of its kind and jerky, inciting Madeleine to sing anew.

She wanted to go in at once. Paul wanted first to take a stroll on the island, but he was obliged to give way. The attendance was now more select. The boatmen, almost alone, remained, with here and there some better class people, and young men escorted by girls. The director and organiser of this spree, looking majestic in a jaded black suit, walked about in every direction, bald-headed and worn by his old trade of purveyor of cheap public amusements.

Fat Pauline and her companions were not there; and Paul breathed again.

They danced; couples opposite each other capered in the maddest fashion, throwing their legs in the air, until they were upon a level with the noses of their partners.

The women, whose thighs seemed disjointed, pranced around with flying skirts which revealed their underclothing, wriggling their stomachs and hips, causing their breasts to shake, and spreading the powerful odour of perspiring female bodies.

The men squatted like toads, some making obscene gestures; some twisted and distorted themselves, grimacing and hideous; some turned cartwheels on their hands, or, perhaps, trying to be funny, posed with exaggerated gracefulness.

A fat servant-maid and two waiters served refreshments.

The café boat being only covered with a roof and having no wall whatever to shut it in, this harebrained dance flaunted in the face of the peaceful night and of the firmament powdered with stars.

Suddenly, Mont-Valérien, opposite, appeared, illumined, as if some conflagration had arisen behind it. The radiance spread and deepened upon the sky, describing a large luminous circle of white, wan light. Then something or other red appeared, grew greater, shining with a burning crimson, like that of hot metal upon the anvil. It gradually developed into a round body rising from the earth; and the moon, freeing herself from the horizon, rose slowly into space. As she ascended, the purple tint faded and became yellow, a shining bright yellow, and the satellite grew smaller in proportion as her distance increased.

Paul watched the moon for some time, lost in contemplation, forgetting his mistress; when he returned to himself the latter had vanished.

He sought her, but could not find her. He threw his anxious eye over table after table, going to and fro unceasingly, inquiring for her from one person and then another. No one had seen her. He was tormented with uneasiness, when one of the waiters said to him:

"You are looking for Madame Madeleine, are you not? She left a few moments ago, with Madame Pauline." And at the same instant, Paul perceived the cabin-boy and the two pretty girls standing at the other end of the café, all three holding each other's waists and lying in wait for him, whispering to one another. He understood, and, like a madman, dashed off into the island.

He first ran toward Chatou, but having reached the plain, retraced his steps. Then he began to search the dense coppices, occasionally roaming about distractedly, or halting to listen.

The toads all about him poured out their short metallic notes.

From the direction of Bougival, some unknown bird warbled a song which reached him faintly from the distance.

Over the broad fields the moon shed a soft light, resembling powdered wool; it penetrated the foliage, silvered the bark of the poplars, and riddled with its brilliant rays the waving tops of the great trees. The entrancing poetry of this summer night had, in spite of himself, entered into Paul, athwart his infatuated anguish, stirring his heart with ferocious irony, and increasing even to madness his craving for an ideal tenderness, for passionate outpourings on the breast of an adored and faithful woman. He was compelled to stop, choked by hurried and rending sobs.

The convulsion over, he went on.

Suddenly, he received what resembled the stab of a dagger. There, behind that bush, some people were kissing. He ran thither; and found an amorous couple whose faces were united in an endless kiss.

He dared not call, knowing well that She would not respond, and he had a frightful dread of coming upon them suddenly.

The flourishes of the quadrilles, with the ear-splitting solos of the cornet, the false shriek of the flute, the shrill squeaking of the violin, irritated his feelings, and increased his suffering. Wild and limping music was floating under the trees, now feeble, now stronger, wafted hither and thither by the breeze.

Suddenly he thought that possibly She had returned. Yes, she had returned! Why not? He had stupidly lost his head, without cause, carried away by his fears, by the inordinate suspicions which had for some time overwhelmed him. Seized by one of those singular calms which will sometimes occur in cases of the greatest despair, he returned toward the ball-room.

With a single glance of the eye, he took in the whole room. He made the round of the tables, and abruptly again found himself face to face with the three women. He must have had a doleful and queer expression of countenance, for all three burst into laughter.

He made off, returned to the island, and threw himself into the coppice panting. He listened again, listened a long time, for his ears were singing. At last, however, he believed he heard farther off a little, sharp laugh, which he recognised at once; and he advanced very quietly, on his knees, removing the branches from his path, his heart beating so rapidly, that he could no longer breathe.

Two voices murmured some words, the meaning of which he did not understand, and then they were silent.

Then, he was possessed by a frightful longing to fly, to save himself, for ever, from this furious passion which threatened his existence. He was about to return to Chatou and take the train, resolved never to come back again, never again to see her. But her likeness suddenly rushed in upon him, and he mentally pictured the moment in the morning when she would awake in their warm bed, and would press coaxingly against him, throwing her arms around his neck, her hair dishevelled, and a little entangled on the forehead, her eyes still shut and her lips apart ready to receive the first kiss. The sudden recollection of this morning caress filled him with frantic recollections and the maddest desire.

The couple began to speak again; and he approached, stooping low. Then a faint cry rose from under the branches quite close to him. He advanced again, in spite of himself, irresistibly attracted, without being conscious of anything — and he saw them.

If her companion had only been a man. But that! that! He felt as though he were spellbound by the very infamy of it. And he stood there astounded and overwhelmed, as if he had discovered the mutilated corpse of one dear to him, a crime against nature, a monstrous, disgusting profanation. Then, in an involuntary flash of thought, he remembered the little fish whose entrails he had felt being torn out! But Madeleine murmured: "Pauline!" in the same tone in which she had often called him by name, and he was seized by such a fit of anguish that he turned and fled.

He struck against two trees, fell over a root, set off again, and suddenly found himself near the rapid branch of the river, which was lit up by the moon. The torrent-like current made great eddies where the light played upon it. The high bank dominated the stream like a cliff, leaving a wide obscure zone at its foot where the eddies could be heard swirling in the darkness.

On the other bank, the country seats of Croissy could be plainly seen.

Paul saw all this as though in a dream; he thought of nothing, understood nothing, and all things, even his very existence, appeared vague, far-off, forgotten, and closed.

The river was there. Did he know what he was doing? Did he wish to die? He was mad. He turned, however, toward the island, toward Her, and in the still air of the night, in which the faint and persistent burden of the music was borne up and down, he uttered, in a voice frantic with despair, bitter beyond measure, and superhumanly low, a frightful cry:

"Madeleine!"

His heartrending call shot across the great silence of the sky, and sped over the horizon. Then with a tremendous leap, with the bound of a wild animal, he jumped into the river. The water rushed on, closed over him, and from the place where he had disappeared a series of great circles started, enlarging their brilliant undulations, until they finally reached the other bank. The two women had heard the noise of the plunge. Madeleine drew herself up and exclaimed:

"It is Paul," — a suspicion having arisen in her soul, — "he has drowned himself"; and she rushed toward the bank, where Pauline rejoined her.

A clumsy punt, propelled by two men, turned round and round on the spot. One of the men rowed, the other plunged into the water a great pole and appeared to be looking for something. Pauline cried:

"What are you doing? What is the matter?"

An unknown voice answered:

"It is a man who has just drowned himself."

The two haggard women, huddling close to each other, followed the manœuvres of the boat. The music of La Grenouillère continued to sound in the distance, seeming with its cadences to accompany the movements of the sombre fishermen; and the river which now concealed a corpse, whirled round and round, illuminated. The search was prolonged. The horrible suspense made Madeleine shiver all over. At last, after at least half an hour, one of the men announced:

"I have got him."

And he pulled up his long pole very gently, very gently. Then something large appeared upon the surface. The other boatman left his oars, and by uniting their strength and hauling upon the inert weight, they succeeded in getting it into their boat.

Then they made for land, seeking a place well lighted and low. At the moment they landed, the women also arrived. The moment she saw him, Madeleine fell back with horror. In the moonlight he already appeared green, with his mouth, his eyes, his nose, his clothes full of slime. His fingers, closed and stiff, were hideous. A kind of black and liquid plaster covered his whole body. The face appeared swollen, and from his hair, plastered down by the ooze, there ran a stream of dirty water.

The two men examined him.

"Do you know him?" asked one.

The other, the Croissy ferryman, hesitated:

"Yes, it certainly seems to me that I have seen that head; but you know when a body is in that state one cannot recognize it easily." And then, suddenly:

"Why, it's Mr. Paul!"

"Who is Mr. Paul?" inquired his comrade.

The first answered:

"Why, Mr. Paul Baron, the son of the senator, the little chap who was so much in love."

The other added, philosophically:

"Well, his fun is ended now; it is a pity, all the same, when one is rich!"

Madeleine had fallen on the ground sobbing. Pauline approached the body and asked:

"Is he really quite dead?"

The men shrugged their shoulders.

"Oh! after that length of time, certainly."

Then one of them asked:

"Was it not at Grillon's that he lodged?"

"Yes," answered the other; "we had better take him back there, there will be something to be made out of it."

They embarked again in their boat and set out, moving off slowly on account of the rapid current. For a long time after they were out of sight of the place where the women remained, the regular splash of the oars in the water could be heard.

Then Pauline took the poor weeping Madeleine in her arms, petted her, embraced her for a long while, and consoled her.

"How can you help it? it is not your fault, is it? It is impossible to prevent men from doing silly things. He did it of his own free will; so much the worse for him, after all!"

And then lifting her up:

"Come, my dear, come and sleep at the house; it is impossible for you to go back to Grillon's to-night."

And she embraced her again, saying: "Come, we will cure you."

Madeleine arose, and weeping all the while but with fainter sobs, laid her head upon Pauline's shoulder, as though she had found a refuge in a closer and more certain affection, more familiar and more confiding, and she went off slowly.

THE DEAD HAND

ONE evening, about eight months ago, a friend of mine, Louis R., had invited together some college friends. We drank punch, and smoked, and talked about literature and art, telling amusing stories from time to time, as young men do when they come together. Suddenly the door opened wide, and one of my best friends from childhood entered like a hurricane. "Guess where I come from!" he shouted immediately. "Mabille's, I bet," one of us replied. "No," said another, "you are too cheerful; you have just borrowed some money, or buried your uncle, or pawned your watch." A third said: "You have been drunk, and as you smelt Louis's punch, you came up to start all over again."

"You are all wrong. I have come from P—— in Normandy, where I have been spending a week, and from which I have brought along a distinguished criminal friend of mine, whom I will introduce, with your permission." With these words he drew from his pocket a skinned hand. It was a horrible object; black and dried, very long and looking as if it were contracted. The muscles, of extraordinary power, were held in place on the back and palm by a strip of parchment-like skin, while the narrow, yellow nails still remained at the tips of the fingers. The whole hand reeked of crime a mile off.

"Just fancy," said my friend, "the other day the belongings of an old sorcerer were sold who was very well known all over the country-side. He used to ride to the sabbath every Saturday night on a broomstick, he practised white and black magic, caused the cows to give blue milk and to wear their tails like that of Saint Anthony's companion. At all events, the old ruffian had a great affection for this hand, which, he said, was that of a celebrated criminal, who was tortured in 1736 for having thrown his legitimate spouse head foremost into a well, and then hung the priest who married them to the spire of his church. After this twofold exploit he went wandering all over the world, and during a short buy busy career he had robbed twelve travellers, smoked out some twenty monks in a monastery, and turned a nunnery into a harem."

"But," we cried, "what are you going to do with that horrible thing?"

"Why, I'll use it as a bell handle to frighten away my criditors."

"My dear fellow," said Henry Smith, a tall, phlegmatic Englishman, "I believe this hand is simply a piece of Indian meat, preserved by some new method. I should advise you to make soup of it."

"Don't joke about it, gentlemen," said a medical student, who was three sheets in the wind, with the utmost solemnity. "Pierre, if you take my advice, give this piece of human remains a Christian burial, for fear the owner of it may come and demand its return. Besides, this hand may perhaps have acquired bad habits. You know the proverb: 'Once a thief always a thief.'"

"And 'once a drunkard always a drunkard,'" retorted our host, pouring out a huge glass of punch for the student, who drank it off at a gulp, and fell under the table dead drunk. This sally was greeted with loud laughter. And Pierre, raising his glass, saluted the hand: "I drink to your master's next visit." Then the conversation turned to other topics, and we separated to go home.

As I was passing his door the next day, I went in. It was about two o'clock, and I found him reading and smoking. "Well, how are you?" I said. "Very well," he answered.

"And what about your hand?"

"My hand? You must have seen it on my bell, where I put it last night when I came in. By the way, fancy, some idiot, no doubt trying to play a trick on me, came ringing at my door about midnight. I asked who was there, but, as nobody answered, I got back to bed and fell asleep again."

Just at that moment there was a ring. It was the landlord, a vulgar and most impertinent person. He came in without greeting us, and said to my friend: "I must ask you, Sir, to remove at once that piece of carrion which you have attached to your bell-handle. Otherwise I shall be obliged to ask you to leave."

"Sir," replied Pierre very gravely, "you are insulting a hand which is worthy of better treatment. I would have you know that it belonged to a most respectable man."

The landlord turned on his heel and walked out, just as he had come in. Pierre followed him, unhooked the hand, and attached it to the bell in his bedroom. "It is better there," he said. "Like the Trappists' *memento mori*, this hand will bring me serious thoughts every night as I fall asleep." An hour later I left him and went home.

I slept badly the following night. I was nervous and restless. Several times I awoke with a start, and once I even fancied that a man had got into my room. I got up and looked in the wardrobes and under the bed. Finally, about six o'clock in the morning, when I was beginning to doze off, a violent knock at my door made me jump out of bed. It was my friend's servant, half undressed, pale and trembling. "Oh, Sir," he cried with a sob, "they've murdered the poor master." I dressed in haste and rushed off to Pierre's.

The house was full of people, arguing and moving about incessantly. Everyone was holding forth, relating the event and commenting upon it from every angle. With great difficulty I reached the bedroom. The door was guarded, but I gave my name, and I was admitted. Four police officers were standing in the centre of the room, notebook in hand, and they were making an examination. From time to time they spoke to each other in whispers and made entries in their notebooks. Two doctors were chatting near the bed on which Pierre was lying unconscious. He was not dead, but he looked awful. His staring eyes, his dilated pupils, seemed to be gazing fixedly with unspeakable terror at something strange and horrible. His fingers were contracted stiffly, and his body was covered up to his chin by a sheet, which I lifted. On his throat were the marks of five fingers which had pressed deeply into his flesh, and his shirt was stained by a few drops of blood. At that moment something struck me. I glanced at the bedroom bell; the skinned hand had disappeared. Doubtless the doctors had taken it away to spare the feelings of the people who came into the patient's room, for that hand was really dreadful. I did not ask what had become of it.

I now take a cutting from one of the next day's papers, giving the story of the crime, with all the details the police could procure. This is what it said:

"A horrible outrage was committed yesterday, the victim being a young gentleman, Monsieur Pierre B——, a law student, and a member of one of the best families in Normandy. The young man returned home about ten o'clock in the evening, he dismissed his servant, a man named Bonvin, saying he was tired, and that he was going to bed. Towards midnight this man was aroused suddenly by his master's bell, which was ringing furiously. He was frightened, lit a lamp and waited. The bell stopped for a minute, then rang again with such violence that the servant, frightened out of his wits, rushed out of his room and went to wake up the concierge. The latter ran and notified the police, and about fifteen minutes later they burst in the door.

"A terrible sight met their eyes. The furniture was all upset, and everything indicated that a fearful struggle had taken place between the victim and his aggressor. Young Pierre B—— was lying motionless on his back in the middle of the room, his face livid, and his eyes dilated in the most dreadful fashion. His throat bore the deep marks of five fingers. The report of Doctor Bourdeau, who was immediately summoned, states that the aggressor must have been endowed with prodigious strength, and have had an extraordinarily thin and muscular hand, for the fingers had almost met in the flesh, and left five marks like bullet holes in the throat. No motive for the crime can be discovered, nor the identity of the criminal."

The next day the same newspaper reported:

M. Pierre B——, the victim of the awful outrage which we related yesterday, recovered consciousness after two hours of devoted attention on the part of Doctor Bourdeau. His life is not in danger, but fears are entertained for his sanity. No trace of the guilty party has been found."

It was true, my poor friend was mad. For seven months I went every day to see him at the hospital, but he did not recover the slightest glimmering of reason. In his delirium strange words escaped him, and like all insane people, he had an obsession, and always fancied a spectre was pursuing him. One day I was sent for in great haste, with a message that he was worse. He was dying when I reached him. He remained very calm for two hours, then all of a sudden, in spite of our efforts, he sat up in bed, and shouted, waving his arms as if in prey to mortal terror: "Take it! Take it! He is strangling me! Help! Help!" He ran twice around the room screaming, then he fell dead, with his face to the ground.

As he was an orphan, it was my duty to follow

his remains to the little village of P—— in Normandy, where his parents were buried. It was from this village that he came on the evening when he found us drinking punch at Louis R.'s, where he had shown us the skinned hand. His body was enclosed in a leaden coffin, and four days later I was walking sadly, with the old priest who had first taught him to read and write, in the little cemetery where his grave was being dug. The weather was glorious; the blue sky was flooded with light; the birds were singing in the hedgerows, where we had gone so often as children to eat blackberries. I fancied I could see him again creeping along the hedge and slipping in through the little hole which I knew so well, down there at the end of the paupers' plot. Then we used to return to the house, with our cheeks and lips black with the juice of the fruit we had eaten. I looked at the bramble-bushes; they were covered with berries. I mechanically plucked one and put it into my mouth. The priest had opened his breviary and was murmuring his *oremus*. At the end of the avenue I could hear the spades of the grave-diggers, as they dug his tomb.

Suddenly they called to us, the priest closed his prayer-book, and we went to see what they wanted. They had turned up a coffin. With a stroke of their picks they knocked off the lid, and we saw an unusually tall skeleton, lying on its back, whose empty eyes seemed to be looking at us defiantly. I had a queer sensation, for some unknown reason, and was almost afraid. "Hello!" cried one of the men, "look, the ruffian's hand is cut off. Here it is." And he picked up a big, dried-up hand, which was lying beside the body, and handed it to us. "I say," said the other man laughing, "you would think that he was watching you, and that he was going to spring at your throat and make you give him back his hand."

"Come along," said the priest, "leave the dead in peace, and close that coffin again. We will dig a grave somewhere else for poor Monsieur Pierre."

Everything was finished the next day and I set out for Paris again, after having left fifty francs with the old priest for masses for the repose of the soul of the man whose grave we had disturbed.

AT THE CHURCH DOOR

HE USED to live in a little house near the main road at the entrance to a village. After he married the daughter of a farmer in the district he set up as a wheelwright, and as they both worked hard, they amassed a small fortune. But one thing caused them great sorrow; they had no children. At last a child was born to them, and they called him Jean. They showered kisses upon him, wrapped him up in their affection, and became so fond of him that they could not let an hour pass without seeing him. When he was five years old a circus passed through the village and pitched its tent on the square in front of the Town Hall.

Jean had seen them and had slipped out of the house. After a long search his father discovered him in the midst of the trained goats and dogs. He was sitting on the knee of an old clown and was shouting with laughter.

Three days later, at dinner time, just as they were sitting down to table, the wheelwright and his wife discovered that their son was not in the house. They looked in the garden, and as they did not find him there, the father went to the roadside and shouted with all his might: "Jean!"

Night was falling, and a brownish mist filled the horizon, and everything retreated into the dark and gloomy distance. Three tall fir-trees close by seemed to be weeping. No voice replied, but the air was full of vague moaning. The father listened for a long time, believing that he could hear something, now on his right now on his left, and he plunged wildly into the night, calling incessantly: "Jean! Jean!"

He ran on until daybreak, filling the shadows with his cries, frightening the prowling animals, his heart torn by a terrible anguish, so that at times he thought he was going mad. His wife remained seated at the door, and wept until morning. Their son was never found.

From that time they aged rapidly in their sorrow, which nothing could console. Finally they sold their house and set out to look for their son themselves. They questioned the shepherds on the hills, the passing tradesmen, the peasants in the villages and the authorities in the towns. But it was a long time since their son had been lost. Nobody knew anything, and probably he himself had now forgotten his name and his birthplace. They wept and lost all hope. Very soon their money was exhausted, and they hired themselves out by the day to the farmers and innkeepers, discharging the most humble tasks, living on the leavings of others, sleeping out of doors and suffering from cold. But as they became feeble from overwork, nobody would employ them, and they were compelled to beg along the roads. They accosted travellers with sad faces and supplicating voices, imploring a piece of bread from the harvesters eating their dinner beneath a tree, at midday in the fields. They devoured it in silence, seated on the edge of the ditches. An innkeeper to whom they related their misfortunes, said to them one day:

"I also knew someone who lost a daughter; it was in Paris he found her."

Immediately they set out for Paris.

When they reached the great city they were frightened by its size and by the crowds in the streets. But they realised that he must be amongst all these people, without knowing how to set about finding him. Then they were afraid they would not recognise him, for they had not seen him for fifteen years. They visited every street and square, stopping wherever they saw a crowd gathered, in the hope of a chance meeting, some prodigious stroke of luck, an act of pity on the part of Fate. They would often wander blindly ahead, clinging to each other, and looking so sad and so poor that people gave them alms without being asked. Every Sunday they spent the day in front of the churches, watching the crowds going in and out, and scanning each face for a distant resemblance. Several times they fancied they recognised him, but they were always mistaken.

At the door of one of the churches to which they returned most frequently there was an old man who sprinkled holy water, and who had become their friend. His own story was also very sad, and their commiseration for him led to a great friendship between them. They finally lived together in a wretched garret at the top of a big house, a great distance out, near the open fields, and sometimes the wheelwright took his new friend's place at the church, when the old man was ill. One very harsh winter came, the old sprinkler of holy water died, and the parish priest appointed in his place the wheelwright, of whose misfortunes he had heard.

Then he came every morning and seated himself in the same place, on the same chair, wearing out the old stone column against which he leant with the continual rubbing of his back. He gazed fixedly at every man who entered, and he looked forward to Sunday with the impatience of a schoolboy, because that was the day when the church was constantly full of people.

He grew very old, getting weaker and weaker under the damp arches, and every day his hope crumbled away. By this time he knew everyone who came to mass, their hours, their habits, and he could recognise their steps on the tiled floor. His life had become so narrowed that it was a great event for him when a stranger entered the church. One day two ladies came; one old and the other young. Probably a mother and daughter, he thought. Behind them a young man appeared, who followed them, and when they went out he saluted them. After having offered them holy water he took the arm of the older lady.

"That must be the young lady's intended," thought the wheelwright.

For the rest of the day he racked his memory to discover where he once had seen a young man like that. But the one he was thinking of must now be an old man, for he seemed to have known him away back in his youth.

The same man came back frequently to escort

the two ladies, and this vague resemblance, remote yet familiar, which he could not identify, obsessed the old man so much that he made his wife come to aid his feeble memory.

One evening, as it was getting dark, the strangers entered together. When they had passed, the husband said:

"Well, do you know who he is?"

His wife was troubled and tried, in turn, to remember. Suddenly she whispered:

"Yes . . . yes . . . but he is darker, taller, stronger, and dressed like a gentlemen, yet, father, he has the same face, you know, as you had when you were young."

The old man gave a start.

It was true, the young man resembled him, and he resembled his brother who was dead, and his father, whom he remembered while he was still young. They were so deeply stirred that they could not speak. The three people were coming down the aisle and going out. The man touched the sprinkler with his finger, and the old man who was holding it shook so much that the holy water rained upon the ground.

"Jean?" he cried.

The man stopped and looked at him.

"Jean?" he repeated softly.

The two ladies looked at him in astonishment.

Then for the third time he said, sobbing: "Jean?"

The man stooped and looked closely into his face, then a recollection of childhood flashed in his mind, and he replied:

"Father Pierre and mother Jeanne!"

He had forgotten everything, his father's other name, and that of his own birthplace, but he still remembered these two words, so often repeated: "Father Pierre; mother Jeanne!"

He knelt down with his head on the knees of the old man and wept. Then he kissed his father and mother by turns, while their voices were choked by joy unlimited. The two ladies also cried, for they realised that great happiness had come. They all went home with the young man, who told them his story.

The circus people had kidnapped him, and for three years he had travelled with them through many countries. Then the company broke up, and one day an old lady in a château gave a sum of money to adopt him, because she liked him. As he was intelligent, they sent him to school and college, and, as the old lady had no children, she left her fortune to him. He also had searched for his parents, but as the only thing he could remember was the two names, "father Pierre and mother Jeanne," he could not discover them. Now he was going to be married, and he introduced his fiancée, who was as good as she was pretty.

When the two old people, in their turn, had related their sorrows and sufferings, they embraced him again, and that night they stayed awake very late, for they were afraid to go to bed lest happiness, which had evaded them so long, should abandon them once more, when they were asleep. But they had exhausted the endurance of misfortune, and lived happily till the end.

LIEUTENANT LARÉ'S MARRIAGE

AT THE very beginning of the campaign Lieutenant Laré took two guns from the Prussians. The general said tersely: "Thanks, Lieutenant," and gave him the cross of the Legion of Honour. Being as prudent as he was brave, subtle, inventive, and very resourceful, he was placed in charge of some hundred men, and he organised a service of scouts which saved the army several times during retreats.

Like a tidal wave the invaders poured over the entire frontier, wave after wave of men, leaving behind them the scum of pillage. General Carrel's brigade was separated from its division, and had to retreat continuously, taking part in daily engagements, but preserving its ranks almost intact, thanks to the vigilance and speed of Lieutenant Laré, who seemed to be everywhere at once, outwitting the enemy, disappointing their calculations, leading the Uhlans astray, and killing their outposts.

One morning the general sent for him.

"Lieutenant," he said, "here is a telegram from General de Lacère, who will be lost if we do not come to his help by to-morrow at dawn. You will start at dusk with three hundred men, whom you will station all along the road. I shall follow two hours later. Reconnoitre the route carefully. I do not want to run into an enemy division."

It had been freezing hard for a week. At two o'clock it began to snow, by the evening the ground was covered, and heavy snowflakes obscured the closest objects. At six o'clock the detachment set out. Two men by themselves marched ahead to act as scouts. Then came a platoon of ten men commanded by the lieutenant himself. The remainder advanced in two long columns. A couple of hundred yards away on the left and right flanks a few soldiers marched in couples. The snow, which was still falling, powdered them white in the darkening shadows, and, as it did not melt on their uniforms, they were barely distinguishable in the dark from the general pallor of the landscape.

From time to time they halted, and then not a sound could be heard but that imperceptible rustle of falling snow, a vague and sinister sound, which is felt rather than heard. An order was given in whispers, and when the march was resumed they had left behind them a sort of white phantom standing in the snow, growing more and more indistinct until finally it disappeared. These were the living signposts which were to guide the army.

The scouts slowed their pace. Something was looming up in front of them.

"Swing to the right," said the lieutenant, "that's the woods of Ronfi; the château is more to the left."

Soon the command to halt was heard. The detachment stopped and waited for the lieutenant, who, escorted by only ten men, had gone to reconnoitre the chateâu. They advanced, creeping under the trees. Suddenly they stopped dead. A frightful silence hovered about them, then, right beside them a clear, musical little voice broke the silence of the woods, saying:

"Father, we shall lose our way in the snow. We shall never reach Blainville."

A deeper voice replied:

"Don't be afraid, my child. I know the country as well as the back of my hand."

The lieutenant said something, and four men moved off noiselessly, like phantoms.

All at once the piercing cry of a woman rang out in the night. Two prisoners were brought to him, an old man and a little girl, and the lieutenant, still speaking in whispers, cross-examined them.

"Your name?"

"Pierre Bernard."

"Occupation?"

"Comte de Ronfi's butler."

"Is this your daughter?"

"Yes."

"What does she do?"

"She is a sewing-maid at the chateâu."

"Where are you going to?"

"We are running away."

"Why?"

"Twelve Uhlans passed this evening. They shot three guards and hanged the gardener. I got frightened about the child."

"Where are you going to?"

"Blainville."

"Why?"

"Because there is a French army there."

"Do you know the way?"

"Perfectly."

"All right. Follow us."

They rejoined the column, and the march across the fields was resumed. The old man walked in silence beside the lieutenant. His daughter marched beside him. Suddenly she stopped.

"Father," she said, "I am so tired I cannot go any farther."

She sat down, shaking with the cold, and seemed ready to die. Her father tried to carry her, but he was too old and feeble.

"Lieutenant," he said, with a sob, "we shall be in your way. France comes first. Leave us."

The officer had given an order, and several men had gone off, returning with some cut branches. In a moment a stretcher was made, and the whole detachment had come up.

"There is a woman here dying of cold," said the lieutenant, "who will give a coat to cover her?"

Two hundred coats were taken off.

"Now, who will carry her?"

Every arm was placed at her disposal. The girl was wrapped in the warm military coats, laid gently upon the stretcher, and then lifted on to four robust shoulders. Like an Oriental queen carried by her slaves she was placed in the middle of the detachment, which continued its march, more vigorously, more courageously and more joyfully, warmed by the presence of a woman, the sovereign inspiration to which the ancient blood of France owes so much progress.

After an hour there was another halt, and they all lay down in the snow. Away off in the middle of the plain a huge black shadow was running. It was like a fantastic monster, which stretched out like a snake, then suddenly rolled itself up in a ball, bounded forward wildly, stopped and went on again. Whispered orders circulated amongst the men, and from time to time a little, sharp, metallic noise resounded. The wandering object suddenly came nearer, and twelve Uhlans were seen trotting at full speed, one after the other, having lost their way in the night. A terrible flash suddenly revealed two hundred men lying on the ground in front of them. A brief report died away in the silence of the snow, and all twelve, with their twelve horses, fell.

After a long wait the march was resumed, the old man they had picked up acting as guide. At length a distant voice shouted: "Who goes there?" Another voice nearer at hand gave the password. There was another wait, while the parley proceeded. The snow had ceased to fall. A cold wind swept the sky, behind which innumerable stars glittered. They grew pale and the eastern sky became pink.

A staff-officer came up to receive the detachment, but just as he was asking who was on the stretcher, the latter began to move, two little hands opened the heavy coats, and a charming little face, as pink as the dawn, with eyes more bright than the stars which had disappeared, replied:

"It is I, Sir."

The delighted soldiers applauded, and carried the girl in triumph right into the middle of the camp where the arms were stored. Soon afterwaros General Carrel arrived. At nine o'clock the Prussians attacked. At noon they retreated.

That evening, as Lieutenant Laré was dropping off to sleep on a heap of straw, utterly worn out, the general sent for him. He found him in his tent chatting with the old man whom they had picked up during the night. As soon as he entered the general took him by the hand, and turned to the stranger:

"My dear comte," said he, "here is the young man of whom you were speaking a while back. He is one of my best officers."

He smiled, lowered his voice, and repeated: "The best."

Then, turning to the astonished lieutenant, he introduced "Comte de Ronfi-Quédissac."

The old gentleman seized his two hands:

"My dear lieutenant, you have saved my daughter's life, and there is only one way in which I can thank you. . . . You will come in a few months' time and tell me . . . whether you like her. . . .

Exactly one year later to the day, in the Church of St. Thomas Aquinas, Captain Laré was married to Mademoiselle Louise Hortense Geneviève de Ronfi-Quédissac. She brought with her a dowry of six hundred thousand francs, and they say she was the prettiest bride of the year.